RICKI
    THANK YOU FOR
HELP WITH MY BOOK
        DAVID REMARKE

Demons

David Remarke

PAGE PUBLISHING, INC.
New York, NY

First originally published by Page Publishing, Inc. 2015

ISBN 978-1-68139-427-5 (pbk)
ISBN 978-1-68139-428-2 (digital)
ISBN 978-1-68289-167-4 (hardcover)

Printed in the United States of America

Contents

According to *Webster*, a demon is an evil spirit or an undesirable emotion, trait or state, whatever that means, and the definition of spirit is a bodiless being that inhabits a place or thing. It really does say that. You can look it up for yourself if you don't believe me, and it seems that each major religion has its own definition of demons and sprits, and that definition depends on what part of the world you're in and what religion is practiced there. That should tell you that they really don't know a lot about them; if or why they exist, and if they do, what their purpose is. Everything that exists has a purpose. People who believe in them say demons have been around forever, or at least as long as men have walked the earth, and that means somehow demons and men are tied together.

In the beginning, some thought there were both good and evil demons, but over the years the good ones seem to have faded away and only the evil ones remain. Hundreds of years ago everybody believed in them and feared them. Today, demons are just something out of the past that people don't think about. And, I almost forgot. Don't believe what you see in the movies. Most of what you see there is stuff they made up trying to get you to spend your money on tickets.

Six days ago I didn't know a damn thing about demons or ghosts. In truth, I didn't much believe in any of that crap, and now I know more about them than I ever wanted. I sleep with the lights on and a gun under my pillow. I have crucifixes in each room and a bottle of holy water by my nightstand. That might be overkill, but I've learned that you can never be too careful.

I'm one of four surviving people. We decided that each of us should write about the events that took place that week. That way if something happens to one of us, the remaining three could get the true story out to the public—not the cover up story that the government was passing out. Maybe this time, the people would believe us.

I'm not much of a writer, so I hope you can get through this. My name is Brett Johnson, and I was born and raised in Church Point Louisiana, same as my parents and their parents before them. It's a quiet little town with down home country people, a good place to live and raise your kids. It's a small farming community where people still say hello to each other when they pass by on the street, a place where everybody knows everybody, and if you want to hear the latest gossip you head to the barber shop. The only time I left home was for the four years I spent in the army, and two of those were overseas. I was in the military police. I liked the work and thought it would help me get a civil service job after I left the service. I saw a lot of death over there, and I was glad when my tour was up. When I got home, I went to work for my uncle who was the sheriff in Acadia Parish, not much happens around here, and that's OK by me. I knew just about everyone so it was a natural fit for me. Life was good until six days ago.

───❖ Day One ❖───

I t was so peaceful that first day, just another hot, humid summer day in Louisiana, who would have thought it would all go to hell so fast. The day started innocently enough, I had just made my morning rounds and was headed back to the sheriff's office. A group from a reality show called *Ghost Finders* was in the sheriff's office looking for background information and directions to the Fred Smiths' farm. The sheriff, my uncle, Charlie Bell, was trying to explain to them that the stories they heard were nothing but hogwash, that Charlie along with the rest of the townspeople had heard those stories all their lives. Haunted graveyard and cursed swamps… he had heard them all. He had even told a few of them himself when he was teenager trying to get in his girlfriend's pants. "I'm telling you for the last time, the stories and rumors are garbage. They never happened, and old Fred doesn't like visitors. He's old school and has been known to chase people off with his shotgun, and he's one mean son of a bitch. If you go out there, I can guarantee that you'll get shot. Is that plain enough for you?"

Charlie had a long history with the Smith family, and most of it was bad. Charlie's older brother, Sam, was Fred's best friend. Sixty years ago, when they were six, there was accident at the farm and Fred lost his arm and Sam lost his life. The story they told us was that Sam got scared and ran for help after Fred got hurt in a farm accident. Sam tried to take a shortcut through the swamp, got lost, and was never found. After two weeks of searching they gave up looking for him, being that he was so young and that the swamp was

7

full of things that could eat you, he didn't have much of a chance. Fred barely survived the accident. He spent weeks in the hospital, and when he was released, he had no memory of the accident. That was probably a good thing; it was a lot for a young kid to go through.

There had also been another incident about thirty years ago. Fred's wife, Sarah, and son, Jacob, were killed by a drunk driver, and Charlie had been the first on the scene. He had also been the person who had released the driver from jail that morning for an earlier drunk driving incident. The guy had gone and gotten drunk again before killing Sarah and her son. Fred was just leaving the barn as Charlie got out of his patrol car and he ran quickly to the house to find out what was going on. Fred and Cassie cried in each other's arms after hearing about Sarah and Jacob's death. That was the last time Charlie had set foot on the Smith farm.

He still feels guilty, and the memory of them crying on the porch haunts him to this day. Sarah had been Fred's childhood sweetheart, she helped him through some bad times after losing his arm, and they called each other soul mates. It was about as true a love as you could get. They were made for each other. Cassie Fred's mother-in-law blamed Charlie for her daughter's and grandson's death, and would carry that hatred to her grave. She swore to herself that she would watch him die someday.

Their passing was hard on just about everybody.

Fred was never the same after that, he stayed to himself and worked his farm. The townspeople did what they could, but nobody could get him to talk about the accident so they just left him alone.

Fred's family had owned the farm for several generations. They were one of the first free black families in the area. They had come from Canada in the middle of the 1800's. The farm was small, four hundred acres, with swamp land scattered throughout it. The swamp and an old graveyard sat in the middle of the farm that's were the source of all the ghost stories came from. Nobody was ever allowed to go back there. Several people tried over the years, but Fred always drove them away. He was pretty protective of the farm.

There were lots of stories and rumors about the place; the kind stories you told around the campfire to get your girlfriend to sit closer to you. I grew up hearing those stories. I don't remember any of my friends trying to sneak out there and check the place out. No one I knew had ever seen the graveyard. Fred's dad, Henry, wasn't as nice as Fred, if you catch my meaning. He was one scary old man, and he always kept his shotgun by the front door.

This reality group was a cable show. They were in New Orleans doing a story about haunted houses when someone told them about a farm on cursed land. It sounded like a good story so they decided to check it out. There were four people in the group. The leader of the group was Ken Marble. He was cocky and arrogant, the kind of guy you hate the first time you met him. There were two other guys, Joe and Tom, who ran the equipment, and a good looking lady named Kathy who ran the video. If I was a betting man, I'd bet that Kathy was banging Ken on the side. The group hadn't been doing well lately. It seemed everyone and their brother was doing a show about ghosts and haunted houses now, and they needed a good story to get back into the good graces with the cable network. If what they heard in New Orleans was true, this would be that story.

Charlie warned them again not to go out there, and then ran the group out of the office. He told them, "Stay away from Fred or I'll throw you all in jail."

After they left, Charlie told me, "I have a bad feeling about that group. They're always sticking their noses where they didn't belong. Swing past the smith farm latter to make sure they aren't causing any trouble out there. Fred and Cassie have had enough grief in their lives. They don't need outsiders causing any more trouble for them. And their leader, I think Ken was his name, he thinks the sun shines on his ass. I don't like him, and I don't trust him. Keep an eye on them and let me know when their gone. Damn outsiders, always messing with the locals. Keep a close eye on them for me, will you Brett? And let me know if they cause any trouble. I'd like nothing better than to throw them all in jail for a few days."

Ken being Ken decided that it was worth the risk. "Besides who does that country sheriff think he is telling me where I can go and what I can do? This is America isn't it, and I have rights," he thought to himself. It would be a decision he would regret later.

Fred's place was about ten miles outside of town. Ken had a general idea where it was, and was sure he could find it with the help of his GPS. They headed out of town following the directions it was giving them. They drove for a while and then turned down a small dirt road. They ran into a farmer who told them Fred lived a couple of miles down the road on the left. Looking at the mail boxes, they finally found the one they were looking for, F. Smith. It looked like time had forgotten about this place. The fields near the road were overgrown with weeds, and it didn't look like any crops had been planted there in years. Barbed wire lined both sides of the long driveway, and several *No Trespassing* and *Trespassers Will be Shot* signs hung from the fence. You couldn't see the house from the road. Not a very inviting place, but the group pushed ahead anyway, and drove fifty yards down the driveway until they ran into a steel gate with a sign that said *Enter at Your Own Risk*. They were just stepping out of the van when a shotgun blast sailed over their heads. They turned toward the blast and saw a tall, one-armed black man with a shotgun yelling at them, "Can't you people read? Get the hell off my land, or the next shot will take out the van."

Fred wasn't much for small talk, so when Ken opened his mouth and tried to explain what they were doing there, Fred fired again. This time, he took out the windshield. It seemed that Fred was in a pretty bad mood that day. When Fred stepped back to reload, he tripped over a rock and fell to the ground, and the shotgun came out of his hands.

The others saw their chance, and took it. They jumped on Fred and kept him away from his shotgun. During the struggle, Fred grabbed his chest and passed out.

Ken, realizing they were in a world of hurt, put Fred in the van, opened the gate, and drove up to the old farm house. They unloaded

Fred near the front steps, drove the van behind the house to hide it, and then called 911 for help.

They came up with a story they were going to tell the authorities that would keep them out of jail. They didn't see Fred's mother-in-law, Cassie, who was sitting in her wheelchair looking out the front window. Cassie had a stroke several years back, can't speak, and has being wheelchair bound since then. She was worried about her son in law and felt helpless watching what was happening to him out her front window.

After the excitement died down the group looked more closely at their surroundings and they weren't impressed. The house was a very old, two story farm house with a wraparound wood porch. It was very run down, and needed more than a few coats of paint to fix it up. This time of day it was hard to see into the house.

Have you ever been to a place that just felt bad? Like something was off? They all felt it, even Kathy.

They had been to some scary places in the past; this place went way beyond those. This place just felt evil.

I was about twenty miles away when I got the call that there was a medical emergency at the Smith farm and headed their way. I couldn't believe it. That damn group of TV people must have gone straight out to the Smith farm after Charlie threw them out of his office. I wouldn't want to be in their shoes when Charlie gets hold of them.

The ambulance was coming down the driveway when I got there. Fred looked to be in pretty bad shape. It seemed he had a heart attack and lucky to be alive. He hadn't regained consciousness yet, and the ambulance crew had him loaded and on his way to the hospital in no time. The *Ghost Finders* group was pretty quiet. After the ambulance left, I took their statements. They all said the same thing. "We were just talking to Fred when he grabbed his chest and collapsed to the ground. That's when we called for help."

I didn't believe them, of course, but couldn't do much about it at the time. That's when Kathy looked toward the front of the house and started screaming. She saw Fred's mother-in-law, Cassie, in the window. She's a very scary looking old lady sitting there. She was bent over in her wheelchair; one eye glassed over and she had a mean looking scowl on her face. Her hair was black and white, and matted. Most of her teeth were gone. I have to admit that she scared me too.

I'd never seen her before.

Charlie talked about her from time to time. He said she was one mean old lady and you never wanted to get her pissed off at you. I went into the house and checked on her. She seemed okay, but was a little worried about Fred. I knelt down beside her and told her who I was, and I told her we were taking Fred to the hospital and would make arrangements for someone to come out and stay with her till Fred was better.

She seemed to know my name, and nodded that she understood me. I called Charlie to tell him what was going on here. Man, he was pissed. It's been awhile since I heard him swear like that. He told me he was on his way, and would be there in about an hour, and to keep them bastards there—no matter what. That's when the next stone dropped.

About five miles down the road, a tractor tipped over and had the driver pinned underneath it. They were calling for assistance. I knew Charlie was on his way, and I would only be a few miles away. Since the situation here was under control, I asked Ken to stay and watch Cassie for me till Charlie got here.

He thought it would earn him some get out of jail points and said they would, so I made a judgment call and left. By the time I hit the end of the driveway, Ken being Ken thought the coast was clear. He knew he didn't have a lot of time before Charlie arrived so they went looking for the old cemetery.

They couldn't get out of the house fast enough. Cassie was giving them the evil eye and it scared the hell out of them, especially Kathy.

Cassie knew they were going to the old cemetery. She thought about warning them about the dangers of the temple and the demon, but decided not to. She thought they would get what they deserved for hurting Fred. She sat there with a scary looking smile as they walked out the door.

They drove down a small dirt path through the woods and swamp that was just wide enough for their van to pass through. Everything looked dead. It was not a place you'd like to be after dark. They pulled into a small clearing and saw the small stone temple. It looked very old, but was nothing fancy. It had a low-pitched wood roof with a steeple in the center of it, and it was about the size of a small garage. It was surrounded by a metal fence that looked more like a cage than a fence. The fence looked out of place here in the middle of nowhere. It was about six feet high and it sat on a stone base that was about two feet high. Why would anybody need an eight foot fence out in the middle of nowhere? This fence should have been around some southern mansion—not here. There was a stone column about every ten feet with weird markings on it that ran to the top of the metal fence. The fence gate faced the front of the temple and had several chains and locks on it. Inside the fenced area there were dead trees that had to be a couple of hundred years old. There was not another living thing inside the fenced area; no flowers, not a blade of grass. Just dirt. It was as if all the life got sucked out of the area. There was a seventy five foot clearing around the outside of the fence that ran to the edge of the swamp and was bordered by a ten foot wide swath of trees. This whole place was will hidden from prying eyes.

They spooked a couple of birds when they drove up to the gate. The birds flew over the fenced area, and fell dead to the ground, when their bodies hit the dirt a red mist covered them and they just disappeared. It was a warning.

The weather was changing. A storm was coming, and a light rain was coming down. It was late morning as they pulled up to the chained gate. Ken was the first one out of the van, and he thought it was strange that there were only a couple of tombstones. "Not much of a graveyard," he thought to himself. He wondered if they were at the right farm and if the people in New Orleans were wrong about this place.

Ken didn't know what to think about this place. It was too small to be a cemetery and the stone building looked more like a garage then temple, but they were here now and they had to make the most of it with the time they had. As they walked up to the gate, the men were discussing what do first. Kathy was thinking to herself that this was a bad idea and wished they would turn around and leave. She'd been with the *Ghost Finders* for five years, and this place was the scariest place she had ever seen. It made her skin crawl. She couldn't stop shaking. She wanted no part of this. She tried talking them out of it, but the guys said, "We've come this far, so let's just finish this before the sheriff gets back."

The temperature was dropping rapidly and the sky was getting darker as Tom and Joe grabbed the bolt cutters from the van and cut the chains that were on the gate. It hadn't been opened for many years, and it made a terrible screeching sound as they pried it open.

The three men walked through the gate and headed toward the temple. The old metal door on the temple had the same markings as the stone columns, and the door squeaked like hell as they opened it. Inside the one roomed building was a stone altar at the far end of the room. There was one cross shaped stained glass window behind the altar that was broken. There were two more single pane windows on each side. Their glass had been broken of them out as well, and the roof had several small holes in it, and was letting the rain fall through. It looked like it was ready to collapse.

Ken figured he had hit the mother lode. This had to be the right place. Even the weather was cooperating; rain, thunder, and lightning was perfect for a ghost show. All he needed was a little fog. This story would put him on top again.

He was right about that, but it wouldn't be in the way he thought.

Kathy was terrified and wouldn't step inside the fenced area. She ran back to the van, crying and shaking, and waited for the others. Tom and Joe got the generator and the rest of the equipment from the van and set up the video cameras and sound equipment. They set one camera on the altar and scattered the rest around the outside of the small room. They tried to get Kathy to come to the temple and help with the video equipment, but she wouldn't leave the van. Normally, she helped Ken with the video presentation.

Ken had never seen her like this. He was putting a blanket over her when he realized she had wet herself. He told her they would be done soon and then they could leave. She begged them to leave now, but he said, "No, there's too much at stake here to leave now."

Kathy started crying again as Ken walked back toward the stone building.

Ken told Tom that the old lady back at the house had really spooked Kathy; she wasn't going to be much help today.

Joe was in the back of the van working on the main recording equipment.

Ken and Tom had stepped inside the temple when Ken started the show by looking into the camera and telling his audience where they were and why they were here. He retold the story of the haunted cemetery and the cursed land that they heard about in New Orleans. He then spoke to the ghosts or sprits that were here. He demanded, "Show yourselves. Cowards. Show me a sign that you're here."

Just then, the old metal door to the building started to slowly close, making a terrible sound. Ken figured it was the wind, but Tom wasn't so sure.

The temperature dropped inside the temple, and a slow red mist rose from the floor.

Tom had seen enough and went for the door which he couldn't get open.

A woman's voice came from the far corner of the room, and asked them, "Are you here to free me? Are you here to free me? Are you here to free me?

Joe was getting great video and sound from the van. After all these years, they were getting real proof that the supernatural exists. He thought it was great until Tom started screaming.

Joe watched the video feed as Tom slowly began floating in the air. Something was holding his arms and legs, but he couldn't tell what it was, and Tom was crying like a baby; begging to be let go. She rose slowly from the ground in front of him though the red mist. She was a very beautiful woman and was dressed in a long black dress. She had coal black hair and eyes that seemed to glow red when she spoke. Her skin was pale white and she had long fingers with pointed nails. She turned toward Tom and asked, "Are you here to free me?"

Tom stared at her and said, "I don't know what you mean."

She replied, "Then you are not the one I have been waiting for." She slowly lowered her head, and several of the small creatures that were holding up Tom became visible. They were light green in color and about three feet high.

They had short round bodies with long hairy arms and tiny legs. They had long pointed teeth and their eyes seemed to be too big for their heads. One creature drove a paw like hand into Tom's chest and ripped out his heart. The other creatures then tore him apart and drifted back into the mist.

She raised her head and turned toward Ken, who was trying to hide behind the altar. He had nowhere to go, so he stood up and told her he was here to set her free, and he had the tools for that in the van. He asked her, "How were you trapped here?"

She said that centuries ago she had been tricked inside the fence by a priest, a medicine man and an angel, and that she longed to be free again to continue her master's work. The door to the temple suddenly opened and they were walking toward the van when she asked, "What tools do you need to set me free?"

He knew then that she had caught on and he made a run for it. The fence gate shut by itself just has he got there, and just as his hands grabbed the metal gate, his body slowly lifted off the ground. He felt something pulling him back toward the stone temple. He knew it was the small creatures had killed Tom.

Joe came running to help him. He grabbed Ken's wrists and tried to pull him back toward the gate. The creatures were too strong for him, and pulled Ken past the metal fence. Just then, Joe came face to face with her and she grabbed his arms and pulled him up tight to the gate and told him that anything inside the fence was hers, and that she wanted his arms. He stared in horror as she ripped his arms off at the shoulders, one at a time. He collapsed, unconscious, to the ground as she slowly walked with an arm in each hand behind a screaming Ken who was being carried back to the temple and through the metal door. Once inside, he was laid on the altar; crying and frozen with fear, he was unable to move. She looked down at him and smiled and said, "You lied to me. Your friend died quickly, but you will not."

The creatures ripped his clothes off. Ken was screaming in pain as they started eating his hands and feet, and then worked their way up his arms and legs. Just as he was about to die, she tore his head off and raised it into the air. She looked into his eyes as the light slowly went out of them. "That will teach you to lie to me human."

Kathy, who was still sitting in the van, passed out. Back at the house, Cassie had heard the screams and smiled as she looked out the window. "Served them right," she thought to herself.

A few miles away they were just getting the tractor off Frank when Charlie called me on the radio and said, "We're just pulling into the Smith farm driveway."

I told him they were loading Frank in the ambulance and I should be back in about ten minutes. Charlie and the two deputies' pulled up to the house and went inside to check on Cassie. Charlie asked her where everyone was.

She just smiled and pointed toward the small path that led out back.

The sheriff studied the old woman's face. He could see the hate in her eyes. Sometimes, the hate never goes away.

In her mind, she thought, "They are all going to get what they deserve: the strangers who hurt her son in-law, Fred, *and* the sheriff, who caused the death of her daughter and grandson. It was going to be a beautiful day!" She watched the sheriff and the deputies drive down the small trail. "Yes indeed, a beautiful day."

Back at the hospital they were getting Fred stabilized. He did indeed have a heart attack. Instead of major heart surgery, the doctors decided to install a stint in the artery that was plugged. I guess, with luck, he should be able to go home in a few days.

Fred kept dreaming about his wife and son. He could see their smiling faces on the porch swing at the farm; he longed to be with them. They looked happy as he faded off to darkness, He kept them in his heart all these years. If it wasn't for a promise that he made to his father, and one that had been handed down from generation to generation, he would have joined them many years ago.

At the little cemetery in the middle of nowhere, Charlie and the deputies pulled up behind the van. He'd seen the blown out front windshield and guessed that was probably Fred's handiwork. He noticed Kathy was passed out in the front seat of the van. After making sure she was OK, they went looking for the others. It didn't take long to find Tom's armless body lying by the fence. He had bleed to death. Not knowing what had happened here, after seeing the armless body, he decided to call the highway patrol for backup.

Charlie and the two deputies pulled their guns and went through the open fence gate. They walked toward the temple. Charlie had never seen this place before, and it gave him the creeps. He had heard about it, and thought that it was an old wives' tale. The place looked pretty creepy. As they walked up to the stone temple, the door opened, making a sickening creaking sound that woke up Kathy. She started screaming for them to get out of there. As they turned toward Kathy, a figure of a woman walked up behind them.

Charlie was the first to see her and ordered her stop. She floated toward them with her arms stretched out in front of her. The other deputies turned toward her, and when she wouldn't stop they opened fire.

She laughed as they emptied their guns into her. The three broke for the gate. Charlie, who was in the middle, knew they weren't all going to make it. As they got to the gate, he pushed the first deputy through. Hands grabbed him and pulled him back toward the temple.

The young deputy, whom Charlie had pushed through the gate, watched in horror as his two friends were torn apart and killed.

I was getting out of my car in front of Fred's when I heard the gunshots and screams. I quickly ran toward the screaming. I was nearly at the clearing when the screaming stopped, and it became scary quiet.

I ran up behind the two patrol cars with my gun drawn. The young deputy was crawling away from the fence on his hands and knees. Kathy had gone into shock and was staring at nothing. I saw a dead, armless man lying near the fence, and that's when I saw her.

She seemed to be floating in a red mist, and was staring at me with dark red eyes, following me as I ran toward the other deputy. I told her to stop and raise her arms.

She just smiled at me.

I pulled my gun and fired. I emptied the clip into her, and I could tell they were hitting the target, but having no effect on her.

She waved for me to come through the open gate, but I was having none of that.

I helped Dick, the other deputy, to his feet and we slowly backed away.

She stared at us and walked back and forth inside fence in front of the gate. She was screaming at us to let her out. I didn't understand what she was asking for and why she didn't just walk through the open gate. As we grabbed Kathy from the van, the woman threw something at us. It bounced off the hood of the patrol car and landed at our feet, it was Charlie's head. His eyes were hanging out and the tongue was ripped out. I fell to my knees and threw up. It was now Dick's turn to help me up. We pulled a screaming Kathy from the van and set her in the back seat of the patrol car. We drove back down the path to the outer edge of the swamp and set up a road block.

By now the radio was going crazy. Everyone was trying to reach us. I told the captain of the highway patrol that Charlie was dead, along with the other deputy, and a couple of others. I had no answer when he asked what happened. How could you explain what I had just seen? He said they should be there soon.

I was gone less than an hour. How could things go to hell so fast? And, what the hell was that woman? I shot her nine times. She should be dead—not laughing at me.

We went back to the house to check on Cassie. She was still sitting in the window with that creepy smile on her face. Kathy refused to leave the patrol car so we left her there, quietly sobbing in the back seat.

We waited for reinforcements to arrive. Dick looked like walking death. I had seen that look overseas. His mind couldn't understand what he had witnessed. I was worried about him—and his sanity. Twenty minutes later, we heard the sirens coming down the road. There must have been a half dozen highway patrol cars, two ambulances, and one fire truck.

John Tucker was the captain of the highway patrol, and was in the led car. I've known John for many years. Charlie and John had gone to the academy together and were pretty close friends. He wanted to know what the hell was going on. As his men set up a command post next to the house, I tried to explain what I had seen.

He said I had to be drinking or crazy, and that he was going to get to the bottom of it. They loaded Kathy and Cassie into one of the ambulances and sent them back to town. Kathy had to be sedated when she saw Cassie was going to be with her in the back of the ambulance her. That should be one hell of a drive into town.

Captain John wanted to check the crime scene and grabbed me and five of his own men, who were armed to the teeth, and walked down the path to the temple. As we approached, the crazy black haired woman was still standing inside the fence by the gate, just smiling at us. I told John there was something holding her inside the fence, and that she would kill anyone who stepped inside.

Captain John said, "I've heard enough. You're relieved. Go back to town and wait for me there."

As I started to walk back toward the farm house, I turned and watched as three heavily armed men rushed through the gate. They made it about twenty feet before the gunfire and screaming started. It lasted just a few seconds. John and his remaining deputies just stared. They'd put enough bullets into her to kill six men, and yet, she was still alive.

She came to the edge of the fence, lifted a torn off head of one of the deputies up so the other two men could see it. The eyes opened and the head and started pleading with them to set her free. She stood laughing.

I was standing at the back of the Ghost Finders' van when I saw that the video recorder was still running. I thought perhaps it had recorded everything that had happened here, so I grabbed the tape and ran as fast as I could back to my patrol car. I wanted to be any place but here. They were calling for more backup as I reached my car. There was nothing more I could do here, and I thought the others were just wasting their time. I heard them mention something about the National Guard, and thought to myself that would be a big mistake. I was relieved it wasn't up to me anymore. I saw the rest of the men running toward the temple as I was pulling out of the driveway.

Death affects people differently. I had seen a lot of death in the war, and you never get used to it, at least I didn't. This was different. This wasn't some crazy man fighting a holy war, and it was something I couldn't explain. It was something out of a bad horror movie. Whatever it was, I was sure that neither the highway patrol, nor the National Guard, were going to be able to stop it.

I remember hearing about a college in Baton Rouge that studied the occult and the supernatural. I thought if anyone could tell us what was happening here, it would be them. I was hoping the video tape would give us clues to what we were facing, and hopefully, tell us how to stop it.

The college was about a three hour drive away, and I could get there a little before five if I pushed it. They kept calling me on the radio, telling me to come back. John must have realized I wasn't crazy, but there was no way I was going back, so I turned the damn radio off. It might cost me my job, but I was more concerned about staying alive than having a job.

I used my cell phone and called ahead to find out who the department head was, and they connected me to Dr. Helen Green. I told her I had an emergency and needed so see her. I told her what was going on at the farm and that I was bringing a video of what had happened there and what we were facing. At first she thought it was a bad joke. I think she heard the urgency in my voice and said she would get her staff together and wait for me. She told me which building to look for, and that she would be waiting for me. I knew I had to work fast. I didn't want any more people to die needlessly.

I didn't know it at the time, but when the guard was called out, they passed the information up the chain of command. After several links in the chain, it had gone to a section of the government called the United States Department of Paranormal Research and Development; quite the name. It was a top secret division of the government that few people knew about. They were created during the Bush years, in case there was something supernatural out there that could be used to hurt America. Can you believe that somebody actually thought this stuff up and the government paid for it? The man who ran the division was Dr. Randall Waters. As soon as he saw the order to mobilize, he thought to himself this was his chance for glory. He wasn't going to let it slip by. His team was made up of mostly ex-military men and scientists. It took about two hours for the first team to be in the air and on the way to Church Point to take over the operation. He left orders for the rest of the team to head out in the morning and to bring the rest of the equipment with them.

Dr. Helen was waiting at the door as I pulled into the parking lot. We introduced ourselves and she asked for the video tape. She wanted to show it to her research assistants and get their input. I filled them all in on what had happened and what I knew. She looked at me and asked, "This is for real, isn't it?

I said, "As real as death and taxes."

All of us watched the video and it became clear to everyone in the room that this was no joke. We were facing something that was very evil and strong.

Helen said, "If the tape is real, it looks like we're facing a centuries old demon. This demon is different from the rest. She's more intelligent and more powerful than the others. She seems to have control of the little creatures, which seems unusual."

No one had any idea what the little creatures were.

Helen had her crew researching the woman demon so we could come up with a plan to stop her. She told me there were several different types of demons and it would take a little time to find the right one.

"You're kidding, aren't you?" I asked.

"You saw the tape, and you were there. Do you think I'm kidding?" She answered.

"OK then, what's next?"

Helen wanted to go back to Church Point tonight and talk to Fred, hoping he could shed some light on what was happening there. If anybody knew what was going on there, it was him.

I told her about Fred's heart attack, and that I didn't know if he was still alive.

She didn't care. She said we had to go anyway. She wanted to head for the hospital to check it out and then check out his home place for clues. We decided to drive back tonight and spend the night in Church Point, and then check out the hospital first thing in the morning. She gave instructions to the team to meet her in Church Point around noon tomorrow and to bring any information they had found with them.

The National Guard had arrived about eight that night and was on site and setting up an outer perimeter around the Smith farm. No one in and no one out, that was their orders. They needed to contain the situation before it got completely out of hand. All they were told was there was a terrorist threat at the farm and their job was to keep anything and anyone from getting out and that there was a different section of the government flying in to take over.

The guard brought all sorts of field equipment and generators, and they had enough night lights to light up a small city. They were ordered to stay away from the cemetery, as that was where the terrorists were holed up. They were a little miffed about that, but orders were orders.

The locals were pissed no one was giving out any information. Country folk are pretty nice people till they feel they're being taken advantage of and pushed out of the way. Then watch out. This was their land and their homes, and they had a general distrust of the government and the way they handle things.

Randall's team had three helicopters with men and equipment, and they were flying in from the northeast. They were circling the farm, looking for a place to land, when one of them made a pass over the temple. As soon as it crossed the fence line, the demon was waiting for them; the last thing the pilot saw was the woman floating in front of his helicopter. It exploded and crashed into the swamp, killing all those aboard. The remaining helicopters landed in the field next to the house, avoiding the air space above the temple.

Randall had radioed ahead and told them that he was now in charge. He was a small bald man with a big attitude; perfect for government work. He was a high level person with an even higher level security clearance. Randall demanded that everyone call him Dr. RW, which of course no one did. He wasn't well liked among his men, and that didn't bother him at all. He became furious with the captain of the highway patrol when he found out that Brett had left the farm with the video. The thought of Brett telling others what he had seen didn't sit well with him. In his mind, this was a national security issue, and he sent two men out to find Brett and bring him back, by force if they had to.

Then there was that damn video. He didn't know what was on it. If it showed the men getting killed that would be a problem for him, if that got out to the public there would be widespread panic. Randall came up with a plan to tell everyone that there was a group of terrorists with chemical weapons at the farm; that should keep the public away, and give him time to find Brett and discredit the video.

He also sent people to guard Fred, Kathy, and Cassie. He didn't want anyone talking to them. He even took the ambulance drivers into protective custody. He wanted a lid on everyone that was at the farm today. Randall was a do it by the book man, with a chip on his shoulder. He wanted a tight perimeter around the farm, to control everything that went on there and an outer perimeter that would keep people from coming into the area.

John, from the highway patrol, got pissed off when Randall dismissed him and his men. They wanted to stay and finish the job they'd started, and to get the thing that killed their fellow officers.

Once the perimeter was set, it was time to check out the temple. He had waited his whole life for this. The sun was just setting, and he thought this was his chance to shine. He walked slowly down the path. As Randall came into the clearing, he didn't see any movement. The first thing that caught his eye was the fence. He saw the fence gate was open, with the chains that had been holding it closed laying on the ground in front of it. He knew that the letters and the fence were a cage, holding something evil inside. He had read that this was how they contained demons in the past, and he wasn't worried about the open gate. He knew the demon couldn't pass through the fence. He saw one dead body outside the fence, and seven more inside. He had his men fan out to surround the fence. They were very well trained ex-military men with a lot of fighting experience. They were all a little jumpy; none of them had ever faced this kind of enemy before. It was going to be dark soon so he had his men bring in more temporary lights and generators and set them up outside the fence line. He wanted to be prepared for an all-night operation, if it came to that. He also set up video cameras around the fence line, along with state of the art motion detectors to capture any movement inside the fence.

The fence gate was open and so was the door into the temple. They noticed a red glow coming from inside the temple, and couldn't figure out what it was.

It had stopped raining. The sky was overcast now, and the storm was moving out of the area, but the temperature dropped twenty degrees in the last hour, and the winds were picking up again. Randall didn't want to send any of his men beyond the gate. He knew the fence was holding something inside. He just didn't know what or why, and he didn't want to risk any of his men to find out. They had a small, remote controlled robot that would do the trick. It had video cameras and sound recording equipment on it, so Randall sent the small robot through the gate and watched as it slowly made its way to the small temple. The cameras were working perfectly. As it approached the temple door, its small arm pushed the door all the way open and then it drove past the door into the small building. The dirt floor seemed to have a red glow to it. There were two more mutilated bodies inside. They all jumped when a small face with two large eyes appeared and was staring at the camera; its skin a pale green. It had very hairy arms and it had small pointed teeth. As suddenly as it had appeared, it seemed to disappear from sight, and then the robot flew out the temple door and crashed in the dirt. That was a first; the damn robot weighed over a thousand pounds.

Randall caught some movement in the sky above the temple. He saw the woman floating about fifty feet above the ground. It was dark now, and she was hard to see with her clothes blending in with the black clouds and night sky behind her, the lighting and rain started again, the lightning seemed to strike her—over and over again—with no effect. She drifted slowly to the ground, her body seemed to have a taken on a dark red appearance, that slowly faded away. It was going to be a long night for the Randall and his men.

She stood inside the fence, watching the men. She would stare at one and then stare at another as if she was sizing them up, looking for a weakness.

Randall made no attempt to talk to her. He wanted her on his terms.

Several miles away Brett and Helen were speeding back to Church Point. It would be well past midnight when they got there; too late to check on Fred at the hospital so they decided to crash at Brett's. He had a small two bedroom cottage by the lake that he had inherited from his parents. Brett called his cousin at the hospital and found out Fred was still unconscious, but doing much better. Then, they made a plan to meet early tomorrow.

Brett's cousin had warned him that a government man named Randall was looking for him, and that they had set up roadblocks to try to find him.

They were wasting their time. Brett knew the country roads like the back of his hand. He had a plan to see Fred if they could make it back to the hospital in the morning.

Helen explained that she was one of the founding members of the College of the Paranormal. They had started it up to do research on ghosts, voodoo, and anything paranormal or supernatural. New Orleans has a rich history of ghosts dating back to slave days, and voodoo and witchcraft go back even further, so it made sense to have a school there. Helen had done several years of research in Europe before coming here to teach. She was considered to be one of the best researchers in the world in the field of the supernatural, and she had a top notch team of dedicated researchers. She looked to be about forty years old, had blonde hair and a nice figure. She said she never married and had she spent all her time writing, teaching and doing research. She explained that as a young girl her family was in the mortuary business and lived next to the town cemetery. It seemed the ghosts took a shine to her at a young age. She was more fascinated than scared, and she spent a long time talking to and listening to her new friends. Of course, no one believed her stories. Her father wanted to send her to a shrink. He thought she was delusional. Her mother stepped in and convinced him she was making the stories up. Her mother had a long talk with her, and told her that she also was able to see ghosts at a young age. She told her it would be better to keep her stories between the two of them. She explained to the young girl that most people can't see or hear ghosts, and people don't believe what they can't see.

Helen said she lost her ability so see and talk to the ghosts when she turned ten. She became fascinated with her early experiences with ghosts and decided to learn as much about them as possible which led to her career choice.

She and her team had been together for many years and had witnessed many strange things. She said actual video proof of ghosts and demons was very rare, and that there were a lot of faked pictures and videos out there made by people that were looking to get rich or trying to make names for themselves. She said shows like the *Ghost Finders* just made her work harder.

Randall and his men couldn't believe what they had just witnessed. How could anything be struck by lightning over and over again and still be alive, and what were those little creatures that picked up the robot and threw it out of the temple? And maybe, the thing that worried them most was how she could float above the ground. This wasn't some damn spook movie. This was real life, and stuff like this doesn't happen in real life. Even the men with the most battle experience were taken aback at what they saw.

After the robot had been destroyed, they pulled back and decided that that was enough for tonight. Randall set several guards around the outside of the fence and felt he had the situation contained. The rest of the men tried to get some sleep in a small tent city they had set up near the Smith farmhouse. After several hours of tossing and turning, Randall decided to head back to the temple and look around. He stood in front of the fence gate and noticed that the place had become very quiet.

She rose out of the ground and appeared in front of him. He was face to face with the demon. It was one thing to read about demons, and another to come face to face with one. His heart skipped a beat and the hair on the back of his neck stood on edge.

He had spent many years studying demons and ghosts, and had an underlying fear of them. It was ironic that he chose this field of work to get into. In his mind, they were always after him. They haunted his dreams at night and lead to a lot of his insecurities. He had an idea what was happening and he needed to confirm what he was facing—and to find out how to use it for his own twisted purpose. He wanted to harness her power for himself.

He had two agendas; one in which he wanted to control the demon so it would do his bidding, and the second was he wanted the higher ups to respect him,. He felt they were always looking down on him.

Randall started a slow walk around the outside of the fence.

She floated a couple of feet off the ground and followed him, never taking her eyes off him. This creeped the other men out, and they moved back, away from the fence.

She was very beautiful. Randall believed that she was a shape shifter, and always chose her shape to suit her needs. He could feel the evil coming from her skin as they walked along the fence. In a voice that was calm and feminine, she asked him, "Are you here to set me free?"

He had been waiting for her to speak first. Randall answered with a question, "What is your name?"

"If you are here to free me, you should already know it."

Randall looked at her and said, "You have many names, but I will call you Lilith. Your name is Lilith, and you are a demon." With that, he turned and walked away before she could respond. He knew at that moment that she indeed was Lilith, and she was one of the oldest and most powerful demons in existence. He was just guessing about the name, she could have been one of a dozen demons that fit her profile. He had gotten very lucky with the name.

And with that, the demon knew that this was the man she had been waiting for.

During the drive back to Church Point, Brett had invited Helen to spend the night in his spare room. They sat in the living room talking most of the night. She told him she thought they were facing a demon, and she explained to Brett that they didn't know a lot about demons. There were lots of theories, but no real proof. For lack of a better term, she said she thought demons were made up of negative evil energy. She believed that everything contained some sort of energy, both good and evil, and that somehow, the evil energy formed demons. She couldn't prove it. She thought the evil energy was controlled by an evil being, some call it the devil, others have different names for it. How could you prove anything like that? The technology wasn't there yet. In fact, there was nothing to prove that good and evil energy even existed. Yet there were all these strange events happening, all over the world, throughout time, and in every religion. She thought that the evil energy could remain dormant for many years till something happened to reenergize it. She said they were years away from having the right equipment to prove this. "All the research I've done on demons comes from different religions. It seems that throughout time they are mentioned in every major religion in the world. Most people don't believe they exist. Their minds just can't comprehend them. I believe something exists. I just don't know for sure what it is, each major religion has some sort of evil being in it. Up until now, it's just speculation. It's going to be a long day tomorrow, and we should try to get some sleep."

Sleep didn't come easy that first night.

Randall had always been a light sleeper, even when he was younger it wouldn't take much to wake him up in the middle of the night. He gave instructions to his men to wake him if there was any more activity at the temple. He wanted everyone to settle in and get used to their surroundings. Normally, he didn't remember any of his dreams. Tonight, though, had been different.

He woke a little after three a.m. to a woman's voice, begging for help. He got up and looked around, but could find nothing. He tried to go back to sleep, but all he could think of was the woman's voice and how familiar it sounded. The thought crossed his mind that the demon had been responsible for the dream. He tried to shake that thought, but with everything that he had seen since he got here, it wasn't that farfetched. It would be the first of many sleepless nights for Randall.

Day Two

Helen and I were up early. We both had a lot on our minds, and neither of us got much rest last night. I fixed a quick breakfast, and after Helen checked in with her crew, we headed out. It was about a twenty minute drive to the hospital from my cabin. I took the back roads to avoid any roadblocks that were set up. We were just a few blocks from the hospital when I told Helen that my cousin, Blake, ran the hospital and would help us get in to see Fred. His plan was for the two of us to dress up as doctors and sneak into the hospital. Once inside, Blake, would accompany us to Fred's room.

Blake didn't like the way the government had taken over his hospital and was ordering his people around so he was more than happy to help us, and being my cousin didn't hurt, either.

Blake was waiting for us with an ambulance and some uniforms. He told me that Dick, one of the deputies, had shot himself last night. He left behind a wife and two young kids. I guess he couldn't cope with what he had seen. He was a good man, and I will miss him. Blake also informed me that John, the highway patrol captain, and three of his men, died in a head on car cash shortly after they left the Smith farmhouse, so that left me, and that lady from *Ghost Finders* as the only two people still alive that had seen the demon, and from what Blake told me she wasn't doing very well.

I don't know if I should feel lucky or cursed.

Blake said Fred was drifting in and out, and it would be a few days before he could answer any questions we had. Kathy was sedated. She seemed to have had a complete mental breakdown, and he didn't think she would ever be the same again. Cassie was okay. She just sat in her wheelchair and smiled at people. She scared the hell out of everyone, including several orderlies who refused to go in and check on her. There were two G-men, my cousin liked to call them that, outside of each of their rooms. They were all on different floors which would make our task easier. Fred was on the middle floor, and we thought we would start with him. We were dressed like doctors and the guards didn't know any different so they let us into Fred's room thinking we were checking up on him. My cousin was right. Fred was still in pretty bad shape. He wouldn't be answering any questions for a while. We decided to check on Cassie. She knew my father, and his brother who was lost in the swamp. We didn't have anything to lose. The guards on the third floor gave us a hard time about seeing Cassie until she came rolling out of the room in her wheelchair. She gave them a look that made my blood turn cold, and they backed away. She grabbed Helen's hand and wheeled back into the room. It was the strangest thing I ever saw.

In the room, Helen kneeled next to Cassie, still holding her hand. Helen smiled at her and told her that she had seen Fred and that he would be okay.

Cassie smiled back and nodded her head like she already knew.

Helen asked her if she knew what was happening at the farm.

Cassie nodded her head yes and then reached out for me. I kneeled on the other side of her and grabbed her hand.

Cassie closed her eyes for a second and pointed to a pad and pencil on a table next to the bed.

I gave them to her.

Cassie had a hard time writing. She wrote that she remembered me, and then she wrote that she was sorry about Sam's death.

She paused a moment, and wrote the name Abraham Judah and that it would be very important that we find him. In her last note, she told us to find a book in the basement of the farm house, and that we would know where to look. She told us the book would give us some answers to our questions about the demon.

The guards were watching us and wanted the notes from Cassie. There was no way I was going to let that happen, just then Cassie wheeled out of the room and down the hallway. The two guards took off after her and that's when we made a break for it. As we got to the first floor, we heard a woman screaming. Something had spooked Kathy. Her guards ran into her room, and we made our way out of the hospital and back to my patrol car.

We thought that since Cassie had given us the name Abraham Judah that's where we should start. Our first stop was at city hall in the records department. Their records dated back over three hundred years, so if he was from around here we should find him there.

The clerk, Mable, was a friend of mine. She had worked for the city for over forty years, and was on a first name bases with just about everybody in the parish. The last name, Judah, wasn't a common name in the area. She didn't ever recall hearing it, so we hit the birth and death certificates. We found records that went back to the early 1800s. We could see that the Smiths bought their land in 1845 and the Judahs bought their plot next door two years later in 1847.

There were also birth and death certificates from modern times dating back to the nineteenth century. We found my uncle's death notice. He died fifteen years before I was born. My father didn't talk much about him. My grandparents told me they were very close and that my dad took his death pretty hard.

We found that the land transferred to the Smith's from the Judahs about three weeks after my uncle's death. We thought that was too much of a coincidence and so we dug further. The census records showed that Abraham sold the land to the Smiths and moved to the Midwest with his wife and son (who was named after him, and was fifteen at the time of the land sale) to work with his brother.

Helen contacted her team and passed the information on to them. She asked them to look for Abraham in the Midwest, and was hoping he was still alive and would have some information that would help them. He would be in his mid-seventies now.

Helen and I decided to head back to the Smith farm to try to find the book Cassie had told them about. We were hoping to be able to slip in and retrieve the book, and leave before getting caught.

From what I'd heard, I didn't trust the man that was in charge at the farm, Randall. I'd seen too many men like that when I was in the service. I knew we would have to be very careful and avoid all contact with him and his men if possible.

Back at the temple, Randall was having a busy morning. He was planning his next move he had his men in position around fence. He knew the safest time to enter the fenced area was right after sunrise. He had his men set up cameras and motion detectors around the temple and fence line. He had all the equipment up and working in order to catch any action inside the fence.

Randall wanted to draw her out, study her, and get control of her. He knew she was very powerful, and if he could control her, that power would be at his fingertips. It didn't matter to him that she was extremely evil.

Randall had been on the edge for years. He was always bypassed for promotions and it seemed he got all the shit jobs. If his supervisors knew what was really happening here, they wouldn't have sent him. They thought a group of crazies or devil worshipers had attacked the sheriff and his men, and that Randall couldn't get himself into too much trouble here.

Randall had the National Guard move back, and away from, the temple and set up roadblocks about a quarter mile out from the Smith driveway. He didn't want them to get in his way, and more importantly he didn't want them to know what was really happening. He was so focused on the temple he didn't care what was happening at the house anymore.

I was surprised that the National Guard let us drive up to the Smith house. The guard thought that Randall had sent for him. We had gotten very lucky.

None of Randall's men were watching the house, and they couldn't see it from their new position by the temple which was well hidden inside the tree line around the swamp.

Helen and I went to the back door of the house, which was facing away from the swamp, and found the steps leading to the basement. It was a typical old basement with a dirt floor and lots of junk and cobwebs. Cassie had said we would know where to look for the book. There was a wood altar in the back corner of the basement that looked a lot the altar in the temple that we saw in the video. That had to be it.

In the middle drawer, we found a large leather bound book. It had the same weird markings that were on the columns of the fence. We had been very lucky so far, and decided not to press our luck any further. We got the hell out of there.

We needed a place to disappear for a while, so decided on an old road house called Happy Harry's, just outside of town. We could get some food and check out the book.

Back at the university, Helen's team had found a lead. Thank God for the internet. Abraham wasn't hard to find at all. He was living in a farming community outside of Chicago. His mother had passed several years ago, and he had become a man of God and had a small church there.

Helen sent two of her team to talk to him and try to get him to return to Church Point. We were hoping he could shed some light on the history of the temple and demon. With a little luck, they could be back in Church Point by early evening with Abraham.

The last few nights Abraham had trouble sleeping and had woken up sweating and shaking. Old memories were coming back to him; memories of his youth and of his father. He knew something was happening on the old farm and they were coming for him. He would have to go back and face the woman demon. He started packing and making plans to return to his childhood home. He had known this day was coming, and hoped that he would finally be able to put this all behind him.

It took the best part of a day for Helen's team to fly to Chicago and find him. They were surprised when they pulled up to his small church and found him waiting for them with his bags packed. He was a small gentle looking man with a long grey beard and glasses. He walked with a limp. He said he had been expecting them, and asked if the demon was awake.

They went wide-eyed and asked him how he knew.

He just smiled and said he could feel her presence getting stronger and he knew something was happening at the old farm site.

With that, they helped him load his luggage into the rental and they took off for the airport. They told him what had happened at the farm, and explained what was on the video and about the people who had been killed. They told him that Fred was still alive and in the hospital recovering from a heart attack.

Abraham said, "I'm going to tell you something I have kept quiet for sixty years. Some of what I'm telling you has been passed down from generation to generation, some I witnessed with my own eyes. The Smiths and the Judah families lived next to each other since the middle of the 1850's. They became very good friends—helping each other out with the farming and the livestock. There was a small temple that was built on a small patch of dry land in the middle of the swamp by the Smith house. The temple was blocked off by a big pile of downed trees, and all the kids were told at a young age never to go past the downed trees. They told us there was quicksand back there and lots of poisonous snakes. Little kids don't like snakes. That seemed to keep the kids out until one day when I saw Fred and his friend, Sam, climbing over the downed trees. I think they were about six at the time. They were just little boys having fun on a summer day.

"My father was just coming in from the field and I told him about Fred and Sam. My father ran down the path and climbed over the trees, trying to catch up with the boys. I followed him over the wood pile and down the trail till I came to an opening where the temple stood behind a tall metal fence. I saw Sam fall off the top of the fence. My father was yelling at Sam to climb back over to this side of the fence. Fred had one arm through the fence and was trying to help his friend when a woman seemed to come out of the ground. She grabbed Fred's arm and tore it off at the shoulder. My father ran up to Fred and put his belt around the wound trying to stop the bleeding. When I reached Fred, my father told me to keep the belt tight around his arm. I did as I was told.

"The woman had Sam by the shirt collar, and was staring at us. Sam was crying, and I was terrified. She said, 'Come and get the boy. He is free to go.' I think my father knew what was going to happen. He looked at me and told me to take care of my mother. He had to try and save Sam. He opened the locks on the metal gate and walked inside and up to the woman.

"I can still hear her voice, 'Silly human, you should never trust a demon,' and with that she killed Sam and my father right in front of me. She let their bodies drop to the ground, looked at me, and started to laugh. 'Don't worry, Boy,' she said, 'you will be with your father soon enough.' She walked up and as she tried to walk through the gate, there was a flash of light and a cracking sound. The woman was thrown back inside the fence. She tried several times, and the results were always the same. She started screaming and ran around like a crazy woman.

"Fred's dad heard the screaming from where he had been working in the field, and came running to see what was happening. He saw Fred laying on the ground with his arm gone. He picked him up, and told me to go home and wait for him. He told me, 'This is very important, Abraham, don't tell anybody what you've seen till I get back.' With his son in his arms, he turned and looked back at the demon. 'I will get them both someday,' she said.

"Henry told her that would never happen, turned and left with Fred. I did as I was told, and went to the Smith house and waited.

"Fred was very lucky that day. At the hospital, Henry told the doctors that his son was hurt in a farming accident; that his arm had gotten caught in a piece of machinery. It took most of the day to get

Fred stabilized. It was after supper, when Henry knew that Fred was going to be okay that he went home to take care of things there.

"He sat me down and told me the secret of the temple and the demon. He told me there was written history about events going back to when they first bought the land in the 1850's, and that he would let me read the book after things settled down in a few weeks. My mother was heartbroken when she was told that her husband was dead. She knew the legend. She had thought that since no one had seen or heard from her in over a hundred years that the stories weren't real. She wanted no part of their farm anymore and told Henry she was going to sell it and move away.

"Henry didn't want anyone living next to him and offered to buy it from her. He explained to her that they couldn't tell anyone that her husband was dead, that it would raise too many questions, so they came up with a story that he was tired of farming and moved back to Chicago to work with his brother. She and her son would follow as soon as the farm sold.

"It was very hard on her. She not only lost her husband, but she couldn't even tell anyone he was dead. There was no funeral, no grieving, nothing. We told Sam's family that he had witnessed Fred's accident and got lost in the swamps going for help. They searched for a couple of weeks, but there are many things in the swamp that could make a young boy disappear. They called off the search and gave Sam a closed casket funeral. When Henry made it back to the temple later that day, he discovered that Abraham's and Sam's bodies were gone. The demon was there telling him that he had to free her. She cursed at him, but he just ignored her. He replaced the chains and the lock, and then slowly walked back to the house thanking God that his son was still alive. At home, he wrote down the events of the day in a leather bound book."

The plane landed in New Orleans and if there were no delays, they'd be back in Church Point by the early evening.

Back at the temple things were starting to get interesting. Just after lunch the red mist came back. This time, it covered the entire area inside the fence. The smell of rotting flesh came with the mist for the first time. It was almost enough to make people vomit.

They weren't visible, but you could tell the little creatures were back. They would move from one area of the fence to the next shaking it. The red mist stopped at the stone base of the fence. It was like water inside of a bowl. Randall was standing just outside the gate when the demon and her little creatures appeared. All the little creatures gathered around her. She called them her children. "It would be in your best interest if you set me free," she told Randall.

"How do you know my name?" he asked.

"I know many things about you, Randall, some good and some bad. Why don't you set me free so we can talk about it?"

He said, "It might happen today. Maybe never, if you don't do what I say." That was the wrong choice of words on his part. Two of the little creatures burst through the unchained gate and attacked one of the guards. They moved so fast the guard didn't have a chance. One of the creatures went high and one went low. The guard was dead before he hit the ground. And, as fast as they attacked, they retreated back inside the fence. It seemed the little creatures had the ability to get past the fence, but only for short periods of time, which must be why they had the fence chained Randall thought to himself. He grabbed a small piece of chain and pulled the fence gate shut. He ordered his men to reinstall the lock on the gate.

All at once, the little creatures attacked the fence, making ungodly screaming sounds. The remaining soldiers opened fire on them. The bullets had no effect. If anything, it just pissed them off.

Randall called his men off. This situation was getting out of control fast. They couldn't hurt them, and the only thing keeping them in check was the fence. Randall heard her laughter in the background, "Are you sure you don't want to let me go?" she asked.

Randall was starting to have second thoughts about his plan. He was trapped. He didn't know if he could control her, and if he couldn't kill her, he was at a loss for what to do. And those damn little creatures... He still didn't know what they were. There was nothing in the rule book about situations like this. He knew demons couldn't be killed, at least that's what he'd learned from his research. He still was hoping he could convince her to join them. If that didn't happen, he would have to try and capture her and take her to a safe location, out of the public's eye. He wondered what type of cage he would need to keep her under control. He was thinking about pulling down the fence and making a cage out of it. The only problem was that if they took the fence down, she would be able to escape; and he was afraid that if she got out she would kill them all. And then there was the problem of those little creatures. Nothing seemed to be able to hurt or kill them. The only thing he knew for sure was that bullet's didn't have any effect on them. In all of his studies about demons, the common elements were that they couldn't be killed, that they fed off of fear and pain, and that they didn't like moving water. Maybe they were wrong about killing them, and if they could be killed, how could he go about doing that. He was starting to question himself.

His men were very jumpy. They fired on everything, and they were wondering if this battle was over even before it began. This was a battle hardened group of mercenaries that wasn't used to losing. The first seeds of doubt had been firmly planted in the minds of Randall and his men.

During the ride to Church Point, Abraham kept thinking about the past and the events that caused him to leave his childhood home. He wondered what he would find there. He thought about his father and the day he died. He thought about his mother and how hurt and scared she was after his father's death, and how she sold the farm to the Smiths just so they could get out of there. He could still see the dark eyed demon lady hovering over his father's body. His father had given his life trying to save Sam. He knew the demon would remember him, and he wondered how she would react when he came face to face with her.

He looked at the group of young people and thought to himself that they didn't know what they were getting themselves into. He also didn't know if he would survive his next meeting with the demon.

He thought he had lived a long life, and if it was his time, he could accept that, but all these young people… They were so young and had a whole lifetime ahead of them. It would be a shame if something happened to them.

He tried to push those thoughts from his mind. The countryside didn't look like it had changed much in the years he had been gone, there were a few more farm sites and newer homes, but other than that, everything looked about the same. He had always loved country life, and the freedom of it all. After his father died, his mother was terrified of living in the country. She felt safer in the city, around all the noise and the people. After his mother died, he picked a small community to serve so he could get back to living in the country. There wasn't much talking going on among the group. They made some small talk about what they thought was happening at the farm site. He just sat and listened. He wondered if any of them had seen a demon or ghost before. They were all excited. It must be because of their age. As for himself, he wished he was anywhere but here, and he tried not to let them see the fear in his eyes.

The young people were right about one thing: the woman at the temple was a demon, and a very powerful one at that. Abraham wondered how excited they would all be when they were staring into her dark eyes and face to face with her. He closed his eyes. He could see her like it was yesterday. He only saw her that one time, and even after sixty years, those dark eyes seemed to stare straight into his soul, and her screams… thinking about it made the hair on the back of his neck stand up. He started to sweat. He wasn't looking forward to this at all.

The old roadhouse where we met was about a mile south of town. I don't know how it got the name, but it's been around forever. Good food, cold beer, and the best part was that it was only a short drive to my cottage. Helen and I pushed together a couple of tables in the back corner of the little bar, and waited for the others to arrive. We had been going over the book we found at the Smith house while waiting for the others to get there.

The sun was just setting when the others pulled up to the bar. The sunsets this time of year were something to behold, each one was different, and we called this place God's country. It was a perfect place to live...that is, until yesterday, anyway. Tonight's sunset was a little different. There was a lot of red in the sky. What was that old saying? Red sky at morning, sailors take warning. Red sky at night, sailors' delight, or something like that. Good thing I didn't believe in any of the old sayings.

I introduced Helen and myself to Abraham, and gave him the book we found at the Smith farm. I asked Abraham what he knew about his old homestead, and he told us he remembered the book. He said that two weeks after his father was killed, Henry, Fred's father, had let him read the book and answered any questions he had. The book started out as a Smith family history. He said that the Smith family had ended up owning the land by about the middle of the 1850's, and that Nathanial and Maggie Smith had arrived from Canada in 1853. They were young newlyweds who wanted to start their new life together in a faraway place. They had the true pioneer spirit, and were one of the first free black families in the area. Their parents were well off and had sent seed money with them to buy a farm and livestock. Their parents had planned on joining them in a few years after the farm was set up and running; they were tired of the long cold winters in Canada. No one knew why they picked this piece of land near the future town of Church Point.

The Judahs settled next to them two years later. Abraham and Annie Judah were a very spiritual family who had fled Europe to avoid religious prosecution. They needed a fresh start in a new country. After arriving by boat, they made their way inland—away from other people and the coast. The Judah family made their living by blacksmithing and farming. It was just chance that they ended up owning the land next to the Smiths.

The two families were about the same age and had become fast friends.

They traded labor back and forth, and they both were very successful at farming. After a few good years, they decided to build a small temple to give thanks for all their good fortune. The Smiths had a piece of land that was surrounded by swamp on four sides with a small trail leading up to it. The land had a clearing in the center and rows of trees by the edge of the swamp and it was big enough for what they wanted to build there. They decided to make the building out of stone with a wood roof.

They made it big enough for the two families to hold their ceremonies there. If they started building in the spring, it would be done by the fall harvest. They thought they could have a feast to celebrate the harvest and welcome the Smith's parents at the same time.

It had taken most of the spring and summer to complete the temple. The two families were proud of what they had built. The walls were made of stone from a stone quarry that was close by. There was one large cross shaped window on the far end of the building and three smaller windows on each side. The stone altar sat under the window at the far end of the little temple.

The Smith elders arrived at the first part of September, and after some discussion, they decided to have their feast the last week of the month. The day of the feast the men set up tables and chairs inside the temple while the woman prepared the food. The families were just sitting down to eat around three in the afternoon, on a beautiful fall day. As they were saying their prayers, the door to the temple opened very slowly and a young woman entered the temple. She had on a long black dress that dragged across the dirt floor as she walked, she looked to be in her middle twenties, and she had long black hair which ran down past her shoulders. The elder Smith rose and asked her, "How can we help you, Young One."

She just stood there looking at the two families.

"You're welcome to join us. We were just about ready to pray before the feast."

"I don't pray to the same gods you do, Old Man," the woman said, "this land is cursed, and you have to leave this place and never return."

"What is the meaning of this?" the elder Smith asked, "You're on our land. You're the one that has to go."

The women were starting to get scared. The men stood up and watched as the elder Smith man walked toward her. "Did you hear me?." He asked, and started pushing her toward the door.

"You shouldn't have done that," she said, and turned to face him. "I gave you a chance to leave, and you didn't take it." She plunged her hand into his chest and tore out his heart as the others watched in horror. She laughed as the man fell dead to the ground.

She brought the heart up to her face and licked the blood off it before throwing the heart on the table with the rest of the food. With a bloodstained face and hands, she looked at the people. Her eyes fell on Maggie, who was heavy with child, and the demon took pity on them. "You have to leave this place and never return. If you are here when I return, I will kill you all. You have till the end of the day to choose." She took one last look around at all the faces, turned, and stepped over the dead body and walked out the door.

The women cried as the men picked up the dead man and carried him back up to the house. The two families decided to stay in one house that night, with the woman and children staying upstairs and the men staying on the first floor to stand guard. During the night, they had decided to seek out a man in the next parish, who they had heard was a very religious man who was wise in the ways of both good and evil. They set out at first light. It was about a half day's by journey by horseback to his home. They found him in his small church, working on a sermon for next Sunday. His name was Samuel.

He watched as the small group of men entered his church with grim looks on their faces, and knew something bad had happened. "How can I help you?" he asked.

The men told him their story.

He didn't want to believe it at first, but he was too old and had seen too many things in his life not to. When the men finished their story, Samuel told them he would come to the farm in two days' time. He told them to stay away from the temple until then. He needed to talk to an old friend and do a lot of thinking about what was happening there.

As promised, he showed up at the farm two days later. He brought an old medicine man named Eagle Claw with him. Samuel asked if they had seen the woman since the first attack, and was told that they had not seen her, but that sometimes, at night, they could hear screams coming from the temple.

"We have a plan to help you, but first we need to see the temple for ourselves," Samuel said.

"Are you sure it's safe?" asked Nathanial.

"I don't know if it's safe, but yes, we have to see it." The preacher and the medicine man walked ahead of the Smiths and the Judahs toward the temple.

"Can you feel the evil coming from this place," Samuel asked.

"Yes, I can," Eagle Claw replied, "It's a very old and powerful evil. It's been here for a very long time." The two men entered the temple. Inside, the tables were still set with food. They saw the dead's man's heart on the table, and the blood on the ground where the elder Smith had died.

"I've seen enough. Let's go back to the house, and we'll explain what has to happened," Samuel said.

It was a quiet walk back to the house. Once there, Samuel pulled out a folded piece of paper with diagram on it. "You must follow these instructions to the letter. You're going to build a fence around the temple. The fence will be in the shape of a cross, with the temple in the center. There will be a two foot high stone base, with stone columns ten feet at their center. In between the stone columns there will be a metal picket fence that will extend up to the top of the stone columns. This is important." He paused for emphasis. "The metal has to be continuous. When you get to a stone column, you have to run the metal around the column. If you don't do this, the fence won't work. The only safe time to work will be just after sunrise, and you must stop before lunch. That's the only time you should ever be near the temple. When the fence is completed, you have to carve these letters and symbols into the stone." He showed the men the proper symbols drawn onto a sheet of paper. "This drawing will show you what letters go where. If you don't follow these instructions exactly, this will have been a waste on time. Let us know when you are done with the fence, and we will come back and take care of the rest. Do you have any questions?" Samuel asked.

One of the men asked, "What are you going to do after the fence is completed?

"That will be explained when we get back. Remember, you have to build the fence just as it's shown on the drawings."

The two families said they understood, and with that Samuel and Eagle Claw left to make their final arrangements.

It took about six weeks to complete the fence, and when they were finally finished, they sent word to Samuel that they were ready.

Samuel and Eagle Claw inspected the fence. Everything had been done according to their instructions. "Tomorrow we start. Tonight, we go over everything that we'll be doing tomorrow. We want both families to spend the night in the Judah house. You must be inside before dusk. Don't venture outside for any reason. No matter what you see or hear, you have to stay inside. Tomorrow, if we don't catch the woman, you will have to leave this place and never return. If you don't, she will kill all of you. If something happens to us and we die, we need to be buried outside the fence line side by side." Samuel gave his Bible to Nathaniel and said, "Give this to my brother if I die, and tell him I have forgiven him and I love him."

With the Smiths and the Judahs locked in for the night, Samuel and Eagle Claw could feel the presence of the demon when they returned to the temple. They knew she would try to get to them during the night. That was why they sent the Smiths to the Judah's for the night. "Are you ready for this, Eagle Claw?"

"This is our destiny," he answered.

The first time they heard her was right after sunset. She stood outside near the front door. The two houses seemed to be bathed in a white light, and when she tried to enter she was thrown backwards. No matter how hard she tried, she couldn't get inside the houses. "Come out and face me," she screamed over on over again. "I know what you're trying to do and it won't work. You can't hide in there forever, and sooner or later, I will get my hands on you." The demon was mad. She was tired of being nice to them. She should have killed them all that first day, and she wouldn't make that mistake again.

She decided to send another message to them; one that would get their attention. She started killing all the animals on the two farms; anything living outside the two houses was killed. It was a terrible thing to hear the animals screaming in pain through the night. The families didn't dare go outside to help.

At dawn, the two old friends headed to the temple to put an end to this. Nathanial told the others to stay inside, and he followed Samuel and Eagle Claw to the temple.

Samuel told Nathaniel to stay back and out of site, and if things turned out badly, that he should get away as fast as he could.

Samuel and Eagle Claw went about their business. They set lighted candles at each stone column. Each man then blessed the fence at each candle, and Samuel splashed holy water on the fence. Nathanial was amazed that each time they blessed an area of fence, the symbols and letters in the stone started glowing. They worked their way around the fence and finally came back to their starting place at the gate.

At first, they didn't see her. She seemed to come up through the ground behind them. Nathaniel was about to yell a warning, when Samuel turned to face her.

"You made a mistake in coming here," she told him, "a mistake that's going to cost you your life."

"If it's God will, so be it," he said.

She wrapped her arms around him and crushed him to death.

She turned toward Eagle Claw, who was still chanting to the spirits.

"They won't help you," she said.

He looked at her and smiled. "You're wrong," he said.

She grabbed him and floated about fifty feet in the air. They were face to face, "Where are your good spirits now?" she asked.

"They're all around you, and your time is at hand."

"Really?" she said and released him.

He fell to his death, and as she floated there, looking down at the two dead men, a bright light formed around her, and an angel grabbed her. Before she had a chance to react, the angel drove her inside the fence line.

The demon tried to get out, but was thrown back inside. She turned toward the angel, "What have you done to me?"

"Welcome to your new home," the angel said.

The demon flew into a rage, and attacked and destroyed the angel.

Nathanial came out of his hiding spot and walked up to the bodies of the two dead men.

The demon stood just inside the fence watching him. "You're going to end up just like them if you don't let me out."

He ignored her and started digging the men's graves.

She kept after him, the whole time; telling him what she was going to do to his family. It took courage to not pay any attention to her, but he would keep his word to Samuel and bury them side by side. He would even go a step further, and block off the road leading up to the temple. He knew he had to keep everybody away, so he came up with the stories about the quicksand and the poisonous snakes. With that, he became the first watcher of the temple.

He started the book which would become the history of the two families and the farms. They decided to keep the information about the demons among the elders of the two families. When the time came, they would tell the oldest son about it along with what would be excepted of him in the future.

Things were fine for many years, until that fateful day when the two young friends decided to explore the land behind the fallen trees. It was all there; in the book.

Everyone was very quiet.

When Abraham finished the story and shut the book, he said, "The last time I saw this book was two weeks after my father died. Henry had me over for supper one night. After we finished eating, he pulled out the book and went over every entry. He wanted me to know what was going on at the farm. A week or so later, we sold the farm to him and left, that was over sixty years ago, and to be honest I would never have come back if I didn't have to.

The book told us that Henry's wife died about ten years later of a heart attack. Fred was about sixteen at the time, and took her death pretty hard. His older brothers and sisters knew nothing of the cursed land or the demons, and they had little interest in the farm. They left as soon as they were old enough. Fred enjoyed being a farmer, and planned to take over the family farm. Before he did, Henry sat down Fred and his new bride, Sarah, and explained the history of the temple. He told his son that it would be his responsibility, and his sons after that, to guard the family secret. Fred and Sarah seemed to take it in stride. Things started to change when Henry died, and they changed again after Sarah's and Jacobs's death.

Cassie, who had come to live them with them, was sitting on the porch when the patrol car drove up with the news about the accident. When she fainted, Fred broke down crying, he carried Cassie into the house and put her to bed. Then he went into the basement and wrote down the day's events. It would the one of his last entries into the book.

Fred seemed to lose his way after his family's death. It seemed that all the good energy and the love the farm once held was gone, and in its place was something that was dead and left unburied. Cassie stayed on and took care of the house while Fred worked the farm. The townspeople tried to ease his grief, but he turned his back on them. He rarely left the home site any more.

One day, he was going to end his pain and pulled the wooden barricade down that his father had built after he had lost his arm. He managed to clear the road and was walking toward the temple when Cassie caught up to him. She threw herself at him, and told him his wife and son wouldn't want him to end his life like this and that he needed to be strong and carry on the family tradition of protecting the temple.

Fred fell to the ground and cried. He was a broken man, trapped in a world he no longer wanted to be in.

The farm fell apart after that, he added more fences and signs to keep people out. He became obsessed with guarding the temple; he even chased a few out with his shotgun.

Fred's son was meant to take his place guarding the temple, but with Jacob's death, there was no one to take his place. That weighed heavily on Fred's mind.

The small group of people sat in silence as the words slowly sunk in.

Abraham was the first to speak. "What do we do now, and how do we send the demon back to hell?"

Helen turned toward her research team and told them they needed to find out why the demon is here. She turned back to Abraham, "Next we need to find out more about the people who trapped her inside the fence."

It was decided that part of the research team would head back to the university and start digging up all the information they could. Abraham, Helen and I would go back to city hall to search for any other clues.

Several locals came up and asked me what was happening at the Smith farm, and why the guard was called up. All I could do was shrug my shoulders and tell them the federal government was handling it. I knew there would be widespread panic if they knew what was really happening out there. I didn't know what story the feds were passing around, and I wanted to keep what I knew a secret, at least for the time being. We were running out of time with that crazy government man running things at the farm. If he somehow managed to free the demon, there would be a heavy price to pay.

Half of Helens team headed back to the university to do the research, and the others stayed to help with the local research. They hung around the bar till closing time talking about the problems they would be facing in the upcoming days.

Back at the farm things were getting bad. Randall was having more of his men and equipment brought in. They should be there early tomorrow morning. He knew he only had a couple of days before the higher ups would take over the investigation. In his mind, he thought he could control her, but in reality, she was controlling him, and with each passing day she was becoming stronger. The more people and equipment that were there, the stronger she grew, and it would only be a matter of time before she could break out of her prison by herself. Randall was a weak-minded man with lots of insecurities. He thought if he could control her, it would make the others respect him.

He walked around the perimeter of the fence studying the markings on the stone columns. He had never seen anything like it. He ran his fingers over the stone carving. It felt warm to his touch, and he knew he would have to understand them in order to control her. Maybe he could duplicate the markings on a cage, and trap her inside. He still didn't how he could do that. He wanted to gain her trust. Maybe she would come willingly, that would solve a lot of problems.

He took pictures of the markings and sent them back to the main office. He was sure they could figure them out, and they had to be the reason she was trapped behind the fence. As he was walked around the fence, she floated alongside of him. She didn't say a word; just kept looking at him. It was starting to freak out some of his men; nothing in the past had prepared them for anything like this.

It was getting late, and he wanted to make sure the perimeter was intact. He knew in the morning he would try to talk to her again, and try get her on his side. He gave instructions for his men to wake him if anything happened. He told them to stay away from the fence and to keep on their toes. He thought that as long as she was trapped inside the fence, his men would be safe. They had set up a small tent city in the field next to the old farm house; nothing fancy, just a place to sleep and get some rest. He thought this would take about a week finish. He laid down on his cot. He fell asleep almost immediately, and then the dreams started again.

He dreamed about being a young boy at school. He wasn't a well-liked kid; he was a favorite target of the school bullies. In his dreams, a woman always came to his rescue and chased and punished the bullies, unlike in real life, where no one helped him at all. Randall thought they were odd dreams to have. He couldn't understand how he could feel happy and sad at the same time. He had no idea the demon was planting seeds in his mind.

Back at the road house, it seemed that Abraham had discovered he had a taste for beer. He had never drank before, and he thought he might never have the chance again—so why not. As he drank his beer, he watched the other people in the bar. He thought it was funny how they had no idea what evil was living at the Smith farm, and that if it got out, all their lives would be in danger. His mind drifted back to when he first laid eyes on her. She was so beautiful, yet you could feel the coldness and evil coming from her. He closed his eyes and the vision of his father's death came back to him, and her screams when she couldn't get out. He would never forget that. He missed his father so much. He blamed himself. If only he had done something, maybe his father would still be alive. He opened his eyes and reminded himself that his father's fate was sealed as soon as he walked past the fence gate. Abraham remembered her words, "Never trust a demon," she had said. He was here now, and he was determined to finish this.

He needed to put this behind him. He had carried the guilt for far too long.

Helen and I were in a deep conversation about what had happened at the farm, about the video, and about how she could just appear out of thin air. "All we know is that she's made up of evil negative energy. We have no clue how she does it."

"You make it sound like she's some short of electrical appliance. Everything is made up of energy," Helen replied, "even evil. The video is the first time we've seen this on film. Until now, we had no idea they could take shape like that. People are going to question the tape. They'll call it a fake. This is going to shake the people's belief in what's real. Most people won't believe it. To them, it can't exist in their world."

After a few more drinks, they all headed back to my house to spend the night.

The demon was floating above the temple watching all the men and equipment outside the fence. She was smiling, hoping that they were going to bring more people to the temple; the more people that came, the stronger she became. All of a sudden, the smile left her face. She felt a presence that was new to her. It was something out of her past, and she didn't like the feeling at all.

She would have to be stronger this time.

She knew all their tricks. This time, she would have her children help her drive the angels away. The demon looked at her cage. She should have left this place after she killed all those soldiers. If she had left then, she would have been free to roam the world where she belonged. "That damn old witch, Gabriele, and the spell she cast. Between the spell and the fence I will be here forever if I don't break free."

Gabriele, in her wisdom, cast a spell that would keep the demon close. She had to return to the scene of the massacre before dawn each day. Gabriele didn't trust the demon. She thought if she could keep her in this isolated location no one else would be harmed. She knew that if the demon got free, she would wreak death and destruction on the surrounding areas.

After a hundred years, the demon knew she was trapped and spent most of her time in a deep sleep, resting and waiting for the right time to escape. Lilith thought that time had come when she noticed the Smiths and the Judahs building that little temple on the site of the massacre. After she killed them all, she would bring that old witch back and make her reverse the spell that kept her here.

In a moment of weakness, she took pity on the pregnant woman. That was a mistake she wouldn't make again. She was just about ready to bring back Gabriele when the two holy men and the angel trapped her. She had spent most of the last hundred years in a deep sleep. The only time she awoke was when the two boys came down the dirt path toward the temple. She sensed their presence and that gave her the strength to take human form. She thought she would be free once the man opened the gate and came for the boy. She didn't realize she couldn't walk through the gate to freedom. She knew the only way for her to escape was to have the fence torn down, and the metal band would have to be broken for her to gain her freedom. That man, Randall, was the key. She would manipulate him into tearing the fence down, and in doing so, would gain her freedom.

⟶ Day Three ⟶

S leep didn't come easy for the group that night. I think the reality of it all was sinking in now. I saw lots of very serious faces this morning. After breakfast, Helen, Abraham and I went into town to do our research there. I had keys to all of the public buildings in town. It's one of the perks to being a deputy in a small town, and it would come in handy in the days to come. In every public building, there's always a room or two the general public never gets to see, and in those rooms there's lots of information that only a small group has access to. My keys would get us into those rooms. They wanted to do more research on the history of the town and the people living there. We discovered that people started to gather around Church Point in the mid-1800s, just about the same time that the Smiths and Judahs settled here. It didn't officially become a town till the 1850s. Nothing special there. It was just a typical town in America.

Helen had her team start searching the death certificates of the 1850's, hoping to find to find more information about the preacher, Samuel, and the medicine man, Eagle Claw. They didn't find anything on Eagle Claw, but hit pay dirt on Samuel. It listed the place of his death as the Smith farm, cause of death was a farm accident, the date of death was about six weeks after the elder Smith's death. The best clue was that we finally had a last name for him, Stone. Kind of an odd name for around here, but what the heck, and with that they did a search on one of the family tree websites and found that he still had relatives still living in the next parish. Armed with a list of relatives,

Helen's team took off to find them. She was hoping they could shed some light on the events that led to his death.

Helen and I went back to searching through the Native American history of the area. Again, there wasn't much hard data before the late 1800's. It was more like a collection of stories and legends handed down from generation to generation. After several hours, they found one story that they could possibly tie to the Smith farm. It had happened some two hundred years before Church Point became a town. In the late 1600s, a Spanish group, led by rich merchant and his son, were trying to get a foothold in the new country. He was a very ruthless man; obsessed with making money. He sent some men, led by his son, to make contact with the natives in hope of setting up some trade contacts. The father and son were very arrogant people, and felt they were entitled to take what they wanted. The young man was not aware that the natives in that area had a long bitter hatred of the Spanish. Once the natives found out the son and his group were Spanish, their fate was sealed. The natives attacked and beat up the son and his group. The son new a little of the natives tongue and tried to reason with them, when that failed, he threatened them; a bad mistake. The natives dragged the first solider out and tied him to a tree. They stacked wood around him and set him on fire; burning him to death. One by one, the men were killed. Watching his men burn to death one at a time took its toll on the young man. The smell and the screams and watching them struggle to get free while they died took his sanity. It was almost a blessing when it was his turn. The natives were surprised that he didn't fight them when it was his turn to be tied to the tree, but the blessing turned into a curse, when they left him there, alive. The natives always left one survivor as a warning to others coming into their land.

When his men and son didn't return, the father went out searching for them. It took three days to find him. After untying him, it didn't take long to figure out that though his body was alive, his mind was dead. He held his son in his arms, told him he loved him, and did the only thing he could do… he drove a knife into his son's heart and ended his pain.

He swore over his dying son's body that he would be avenged. It took some time, but he tracked the natives back to their camp and attacked them. The natives were no match for the larger group of well-armed soldiers, and most of them were killed. When they were done with the killing, they stacked all the bodies in a pile and set them on fire. The fire burned most of the day, and the smell of death was everywhere.

A small group of survivors managed to escape inland. They had gone to a place that they considered sacred, a place where their ancestors held all their ancient ceremonies. They thought they would be safe there, and that the spirits of their ancestors would protect them. This sacred place was on small piece of dry land surrounded by swamp on all sides. The ancestors had built a small dirt path to the dry land, where they could have all their sacred ceremonies. It had been many generations since anyone had visited this place.

One of the survivors was the witch, Gabriele. Her mother and grandmother were witches before her. She was held in high esteem in the eyes of the tribe. She healed the sick, cast spells on all her people's enemies, and was sought out for advice on everything from when to conceive to what types of crops to plant.

Gabriele had seen her mother, her young daughter, and the tribe's elders killed in the first attack. She knew that she would be the last in her family's line of witches. She was sure it also meant the end of the line for her tribe. Every night since their deaths she prayed to the ancient gods of the dark to avenge their deaths. She knew she would have to be patient.

They lived in peace for several years. The dead son's father never gave up the search for the remaining natives. He wanted them all dead. When he finally found them, he sent his men to finish the job.

The soldiers were brutal. They killed every living thing in the camp, men, women and children, and animals. The last one alive was Gabriele. She was chanting and praying. When they came up behind her, she stood and faced her attackers. She told them in her native tongue that they were all going to die a terrible death today, and none would be left alive by sunset. There were two soldiers that spoke her language. They told the father what she had said, he looked at her and told her, "This was all you're doing." He took out his knife and cut her throat, "This is for my son." He let her body drop to the ground.

According to the legend, the sky became overcast and a red mist started rising from the ground. Then a figure of a woman appeared in the middle of the men, the men started to panic and move away from her. She was quiet for a minute as she looked around at all the dead natives. She raised her hands, and several creatures of the night appeared through the mist and attacked and killed the screaming men. There was no defense against her. Soon, all were dead, except for the father who was standing there with the blood on his hands. All of the little creatures surrounded him. The woman seemed to float toward the father and slowly walked around him. She looked into his eyes, slowly tore his head off, and threw it into the swamp.

The demon wandered through the camp for hours in the red mist till she found the body of the dead witch. She picked her up, and sank back into the red mist, and when the red mist had disappeared all of the bodies of the natives were gone. It didn't take long for the remaining bodies to rot in the hot summer sun. After the massacre, she became something of a folk hero to the natives. The story had been passed down from generation to generation of the native people. The land description matched the temple site at the Smith farm. the description of the woman that killed the soldiers matches the woman at the farm, and even the little creatures sounded the same. It had to be the same demon that was summoned by Gabriele back in the 1600's. It was starting to look like the Smith and the Judah families had the bad luck to settle on the same site where the massacre had happened. Fate can be a bitch sometimes.

And the chances of them building a religious temple on the same spot where all that blood was shed were just unbelievable.

They found another story about an old medicine man who had died battling an evil spirit in the middle of the 1800's.

The group at the university wasn't having much luck. They found stories about the markings on the stone columns, which said that they had appeared in small settings all around the world, and in different times, which didn't make any sense. The symbols were always the same. No one had ever been able to determine who made the markings or what they meant. The strange thing about the markings was that they were always in stone and seemed to encircle a small building or structure. They had a little more luck with the natives.

It seemed they believed and practiced a form of black magic. They had many different gods that they believed in. They prayed for good weather, large crops, large families, and peace. They had also been known to sacrifice small animals from time to time when things got really bad. There still were many questions left to be answered. The main ones were why that demon, why was it still here, and how do we get rid of it?

According to Helen, there were many different types of demons; each one had its own name and powers. No one really knows what they are, or were they come from. Some believe that demons are created by the devil, sent to roam the earth to try to shake up people's faith in God.

I asked Helen, "Are you sure it's a demon? I came face to face with her and she looks too good to be one."

Helen laughed and said, "You've been watching too much late night TV. In my studies, I found that demons can look like your next door neighbor, so they can fit in anyplace, and most of them don't have horns or big eyes and long fingernails." She went on to say, "Most evil things could be standing right next to you, and you wouldn't even notice them. There are many stories about all kinds of demons, from all parts of the world. Many people don't believe in them because the stories are so hard to prove, most believe that some people just go crazy and do terrible things to other people.

Some believe that demons can possess a human body and make them due terrible things. It's hard to tell where the truth is. I believe that evil does evil things in some form or another. We're just beginning to scratch the surface about demons, and we have a long way to go before we understand what they really are."

Back at the farm Randal was spending most of the morning setting up his command post and going over the events of the last three days. After another night filled with bad dreams, he was having trouble getting focused. He was tired of the guard. They were always asking questions. He felt they were trying to work their way in to take over. He would have none of that. He decided to push the guard even further back. He didn't want any more interference from them. The guard wasn't happy playing second fiddle to the feds, and they voiced their displeasure to him. His response was that he was in charge, and they could either move back or be replaced.

Randall spent some time studying the strange markings on the stone. He had never seen the symbols before, and they seemed out of place in this part of the country. He thought the strange symbols were the key to keeping the demon locked up inside the fence. He wondered if they were some sort of ancient language. Maybe it was the language of the demons and they were bound by writing. Who knew, but for the first time since he got here, he was starting to feel a little better about the situation at the farm. He also noticed that the metal fence between the stone columns was continuous. When the metal fence got to a stone column there was a piece of metal that wrapped around the column and tied into the next section of metal fence. It was like the metal fence was one piece. He once read a story about how demons and metal don't mix. Some say the metal holds some strange spell over them, and they avoid it at all costs. Between the metal fence, the stone columns, and the swamp surrounding the temple, it formed the perfect prison for the demon. Randall had a day to think about his idea about trapping her, and had decided it would be impossible without knowing what the symbols stood for. She was just too powerful, and she had her little creatures to help her.

He figured if she had the chance, she would kill him and all his men. She would have to come willingly or not at all.

The demon and the little creatures always seemed to appear about mid-afternoon. Today had been a little different. There was no red mist today, and no little creatures. When the demon appeared, it seemed as if she was waiting for someone or something.

Randall's men were getting a little jumpy, and every time she got near one, she would come right up to the fence and stare at them until they backed away. They are all weak little men, she thought to herself. I will make them all pay for keeping me here.

Randall's supervisors had called and wanted a progress report. Randall informed them that things were fine, and he should have it wrapped up in four or five days. His superiors were hoping that this would be the end of the line for him, and that he would screw up so badly that they could get rid of him. They would soon get their wish. As Randall walked back toward the temple, he was feeling the pressure. He knew this was his last chance to attain something that had always eluded him.

He came into the opening and watched the demon float toward the sky. She seemed to spin as she came to a stop about fifty feet above the ground. All the men were watching her as she moved away from the center of the fenced area. When she got to the fence line, she stopped and reached out with her hand. When her hand touched the fence, the sky lit up, and for a second, you could see the outline of the cage that was holding her. It seemed to go straight up, as far as the eye could see. She moved a few feet away and tried again. Every time she touched the fence, some unknown force threw her back, and that seemed to piss her off. It looked like she was looking for a weak spot. She tried over and over again, and spent most of the afternoon looking. She seemed to be getting stronger as she went. As Randall watched, this began to worry him. What if she got out? He thought to himself that she would kill them all, and there was no telling what she would do to the locals; not that he cared for them, anyway. He was more worried about the effect it would have on his career.

It was early afternoon when the rest of Randall's men and equipment showed up. It was a nice distraction for Randall. It helped him forget about the demon for a while. After the trucks were unloaded, they had a small briefing about what was happening. The new arrivals didn't know what to think. They would soon find out what real evil was.

Helen's team wasn't having much luck at finding Samuel's relatives, until they stopped to fill their car with gas and asked the attendant if he knew if there were any Stones living nearby.

"What do you want with them?" he asked.

"We're doing research on a Samuel Stone from the 1850's. We're writing a book about him and the events that happened at the Smith farm." Sometimes you have to lie a little to get what you need.

"How do you know what happened there?" the young man asked.

"Like I said, we're writing a book about him, and all our research tells us he has relatives living in this area."

"You're in luck," said the young man. "My last name is Stone, and Samuel was related to me. This is what you need to do… pick up a couple bottles of Jack Daniels, and go to this address. It's my great-grandfather's house. He knows more about Samuel than anybody. He's a little hard of hearing, so you have to speak loud when you talk to him. First, tell him that Cody sent you. That's me. He doesn't like strangers. When you tell him I sent you, hand him the two bottles of Jack. If he smiles, you're home free. If not, run as fast as you can. Grandma doesn't like it when he drinks, but what the hell, he's one hundred and two, and in my book, he's entitled.

"Take the next left and drive about a mile. Remember what I told you, now."

The first words out of their mouths were, "Where is the nearest liquor store?"

As they pulled up to the address, they notice a very old man sitting on the front porch in a rocking chair, and of course, he had a shotgun standing next to him.

"I don't know if I want to go up there," one of them said. "I'll go first. Keep the car running just in case."

"You boy's ain't selling anything, are you?"

"No, sir. Cody sent us." And then they handed the two bottles of Jack to the old man.

He smiled and said, "That Cody is a good boy. What can I do for you?"

"We're writing a book about Samuel Stone, and Cody said you were the man to see."

"Tell your friends they can turn off your car and join us. This will take a while." He noticed the young man looking at the shotgun, and said, "Don't worry about that, Son, my daughter hid all the shells. Damn woman takes all the fun out of life, if you know what I mean. And before you sit down, go into the kitchen and get some glasses. We're going to do a little drinking. And hide that second bottle in the cabinets by the sink so she won't find it. She stops looking when she finds the first bottle, that's why Cody always sends two. He's a smart boy, that Cody. I love my daughter, but sometimes, she can be a pain in the ass.

"My name is Will, not sir or mister. Do you understand?"

They all nodded their heads.

"I almost forgot. Will one of you go in the front room, and underneath the cross on the far wall you'll find a large Bible, will you bring it to me please? My knees aren't as good as they used to be."

As they were bringing it to him, he said, "This was Samuel's Bible. Samuel was my great, great grandfather. I was born in nineteen hundred and ten, or maybe eleven. I guess that part doesn't matter much. Samuel grew up in a big family, as was the custom back then. The children were needed to help around the farm. They depended on one and another to get by. Samuel thought he would end up on the farm, and that was okay. When he was about fifteen, he went swimming down at the lake. Summers can be awful hot around here. Anyway, he was by himself that day, and said he started to get the cramps and tried to make it to shore. He didn't make it. He thought he was going to die that day. He was just about gone when he felt a pair of hands grab him and pull him to shore. After a few minutes of coughing up water, he looked up and saw a smiling native boy looking down at him. "I think you're going to live," he told Samuel and then reached down and helped him to his feet.

The young man's name was Eagle Claw, and the two boys were about the same age. Eagle Claw told Samuel that the water spirit told him Samuel was in trouble, and that it wasn't his time or destiny to die like that. The boys became fast friends and talked about spiritual things. Samuel ended up wanting to become a man of God, which caused problems between him and his brothers. Soon after, Samuel left to join the church. He spent four years studying religion, and on the fifth year, they turned him loose on the world to make his own way. Through all these years, Eagle Claw had remained a true friend, and had become a medicine man. The church sent Samuel back to his home town to build a church. The church was Samuel's pride and joy. The county donated the land, and all the local farmers and their families helped build it. People called it the Sunrise Country Church. Samuel liked that name." He paused a moment before going on. "It's best if you take a drink or two before I go any farther. I didn't believe much of what I'm about to tell you at first. Neither did my dad, until we made a visit to the Smith farm."

He opened up Samuel's Bible. "It says in here that one day, when he was working in his church two families came to visit him, it was the Smiths and the Judahs. They told him what had happened the day before at the celebration, and how the woman had appeared and killed the Smith elder. Samuel didn't quite know how to take this, at first he didn't believe them, but the look in their eyes told him they were all very scared. He decided he would have to see this place before making any decisions on how to proceed.

"After they left for home, Samuel headed over to Eagle Claw's home. He knew he would need his help with this. Samuel and Eagle Claw had heard a very similar story before. As young men, they sat and listened to old native legends, and one of his favorites was the story of Gabriele and how she summoned a demon to take revenge for her people's murder. 'Do you think it's the same demon asked Samuel?' Eagle Claw told him, "The only one way to know for sure would be to go there and see for ourselves.'

"The two made plans to leave at first light. Samuel had a restless night, he decided that it was useless trying to sleep so he got up and started a fire and sat in his favorite chair to think about how they were going to handle the demon at the Smith farm. He had just nodded off a little after midnight when he woke to see an angel standing in front of him. He thought he was dreaming. 'I'm here to help you,' said the angel.

"The angel went on to tell him that they needed to build a fence around the temple. He explained how the fence was to be made and what to do when the fence was complete. He told Samuel that they were facing a centuries old demon; one of the most powerful ones. The angel told him the price would be very high to capture the demon, and that price would likely be their lives. He went on to say that the safest time to work was when the demon was at rest. The angel said that he would be back when the fence was complete, and with that, the angel was gone.

"Samuel and Eagle Claw met after first light and headed to the Smith farm. Samuel told Eagle Claw about the visitor he had the night before, and Eagle Claw said that a spirit had come to him as well, and had told him basically the same things.

"They reached the farm around midday. The two families were very happy to see them.

"Samuel wanted to see the temple before it got too late, and so he told the families to stay in the house and that only he and Eagle Claw would go to the temple today.

"The two men headed down the dirt path toward the temple, and with each step they could feel the evil getting stronger. Eagle Claw said, 'This is not a good place.'

"They made their way to the temple. As they were leaving the clearing heading, toward the temple, Eagle Claw turned back and just for a second, he saw a dark haired woman standing near the temple door.

"Back at the house Samuel, told the families how to build the fence. When the families asked what the letters meant, he told them, 'It doesn't matter. It just has to be done this way. Eagle claw and I will help you lay out the fence in the morning before we go. Do you have any questions?'

'What is that woman that killed my father?'

'She's a very old and powerful demon,' Samuel answered.

'Why is she here?'

'That's one question we don't have the answer to. All we know is she's here now, and we have to deal with it. I think we all should turn in. It's going to be a long day tomorrow.'

"Samuel was the first to rise the next morning, with the rest following soon after. It took most of the morning to lay out the fence and go over how they were to proceed. The two men said their goodbyes and started for home to wait for word that the fence was finished, and to know when they should return.

"It took five weeks to complete the fence and another week to carve the symbols and letters into the stone.

"Samuel and Eagle claw had spent the last few weeks getting ready for the end. They knew death was waiting for them. Samuel spent a lot of time writing letters to his family, telling them how much he loved them and that he forgave them for the way they had treated him years ago. In the letter to his older brother, he asked if he would look after his church. He told him that he was giving all he had to him, including his Bible that their father had given to him when he was a young boy.

"Eagle Claw spent a lot of his time at the gravesite of his grandfather. He was the man whom he had loved the most in this world. He spent days telling him about his life, and of the demon and the plan they had come up with to capture her. On the day the fence was complete, he said his last goodbye to his beloved grandfather. Samuel waited just outside the burial grounds for his old friend.

'Are you ready for this? This is our destiny, my friend,' said Eagle Claw.

"As they headed to the Smith farm, they went over the plan. The angel had explained that sacrifices would have to be made in order to succeed. The plan was to distract the demon, and then drive her past the fence line. Once inside, she wouldn't be able to leave. The angel had told both men that there was a good chance they would both be killed, and that if the demon wasn't trapped, she would kill and terrorize everyone in the small community.

"Both men felt more at peace with the world, than any time in their past. They really had no choice in the matter, even at the risk of death. It was mid mourning when the two reached the Smith farm. They walked slowly toward the temple. They could feel her presence, the presence of evil. Overnight, all the grass and trees near the temple had died, and then there was the smell… It was the smell of death.

"The two men inspected the fence. Everything was as the angel had requested. They spent the night at the Smith house. They would wait till morning to bless the fence and set the trap.

"Samuel gave his Bible and his letters to the Smith family with his instructions to give it to his brother. He told them sternly that no matter what they saw or heard, they could not leave the house."

Will looked over the young people he was telling the story to and said, "The next entry in Samuels's Bible is from Nathanial Smith. He wrote the last day's events in it before he returned the Bible to Samuels's brother. It was a long sleepless night for all of them. The morning sun seemed to take forever to get there, and when it finally came, the two very tired old man walked down the dirt path toward the temple.

"Nathanial told the rest of his family to stay in the Judah home till it was all over, he followed Samuel and Eagle Claw to the temple. Samuel told him he could only stay if he stayed back and hidden out of the way. He agreed to that, and watched as Samuel and Eagle Claw lit candles at each stone column around the fence, and blessed the fence.

"While they were blessing the last section a woman's voice came from behind them, 'You can't hurt me with that,' she said.

"Samuel turned toward her and told her it was not meant to hurt her. The two men completed their work, before she finally had enough and attacked Samuel. She wrapped her arms around him and slowly crushed him to death. Then she turned her attention to Eagle Claw.

"'You should have known better than to come to this place,' Eagle Claw said. 'This is a sacred place of my ancestors. I belong here, and you don't.'

"'I wouldn't be here now if it wasn't for that damned old witch and her curse. You, of all people, should have known better than to challenge me.' With that she wrapped her arms around him and floated into the air. 'Where are you ancestors now, and why aren't they here to help you?'

"Eagle Claw said, 'They are here and there, all around you.'

"She didn't like his answer. She opened her arms and dropped the medicine man to his death. As she looked down on the two dead men, she thought that in all the time she had roamed the earth, these were the first two men who had showed no fear as they died. It was time to make her way to the farmhouses and take care of the others, but she was surprised by a bright light. An angel stepped out of the light, grabbed her, and forced her inside the fence line before she could react.

"'What have you done?' she screamed and tried to fly away. She was thrown back inside with a flash of light.

"'It's no use,' the angel said to her. 'You can never cross the fence line.'

"The demon turned toward the angel and attacked. The angel fought back, but in the end was destroyed by the demon.

"Nathanial was terrified at what he had just witnessed. He must have sat there for hours before he got up the courage to check on Samuel and Eagle Claw. He knew they were both dead. He honored Samuel's last wishes and buried the two men side my side outside the fence. The tombstones would come later. The demon kept screaming at him while he buried the men, she told him, 'I'm going to kill you and your family if you don't free me!'

"Nathaniel didn't pay any attention to her and kept working. He decided that he was going to have to block the road to keep people out. He cut down some trees and lay them over the road. It took a couple of days to stack the trees high enough to keep people out.

"That first week was the worst for the Smiths. They could hear the demon screaming each night. But, for each night that went by, the sound of her screaming faded away a bit, and by the end of the week the sound had stopped completely.

"Nathanial returned Samuel's Bible to his brother. After reading the letter that Samuel had sent to him and all the stories written in the Bible, he finally understood what kind of man his brother was. He felt ashamed at how the family had treated Samuel all those years. He cried and wished he could have told his brother that he loved him, that he was very proud of his brother's work, and that he would be honored to look after Samuel's church.

"Nathanial gathered that two families and explained to them that no outsiders could ever learn the secret of the temple and that it would up to the families to keep people out. He came up with the story that the road had been blocked because of quicksand and poisonous snakes. And the story worked for over a hundred years."

Will looked at the group of speechless young people, "That's quite a story isn't it? And there's more. When Nathanial brought Samuel's Bible to his brother, he told him that there may come a day when the demon gets out, and when that day comes, some people would come looking for answers. If they came, the family was supposed to give them Samuel's Bible. I guess that day is today, isn't it?"

They nodded yes.

"Is the demon out?" he asked.

"Not yet," they told him, "but it would be just a matter of days till she was free."

"The Bible really belongs with Nathanial's book. Together they tell the whole story of what happened at the farm. Please take good care of it for me." He handed the Bible over to them, shook each of their hands, and wished them luck. As they were walking back to their car he yelled, "If I was ten years younger, I'd be going back with you."

No one in the group doubted him.

The old man watched as the group of young people got in their car and left. He wished he could have gone with them, but his body was well past its prime, and he knew he wouldn't be much help to them. He decided to lay off the booze for a few days and have his shotgun ready, just in case that damn demon got free. He knew where his daughter had hid the shells. As the young people drove away, he silently said a prayer for them.

The old Bible was quite a find. The young people were surprised when the old man gave it to them. Armed with the Bible, they headed back to Church Point to pass the new information on to Helen.

Abraham spent some time looking around his old town. Things were pretty much the same. There was a new hospital and town library, but other than that, not much had changed. He was glad that the park was still in the center of town. He had spent a lot of time there when he was a kid. It had brought back many good memories of a better time.

He had Brett take him to the old cemetery where most of his relatives were buried. There was no grave for his father. Why would there be? Everyone thought he had gone to Chicago to be with his brother. Abraham thought that if he survived this, he would fix that and give his father a decent funeral and burial. He deserved that.

He spent some time praying and reflecting on his life. He wondered if his father would be proud of him. He had spent his whole life trying to live up to his father's name.

They headed back to the old roadhouse to meet with Helen's team to go over what they had found and try to come up with a plan to stop the demon.

Things had gotten interesting at the roadhouse. Randall had heard it was one of my hangouts, and so took two of his men and headed there.

I was easy to spot. He still had his deputy's uniform on. Randall and his men walked up behind him. The whole bar got deadly quiet. I stood up, faced the men, and smiled.

Randall saw the smile and looked behind him. There were at least twenty locals walking toward them.

"That's far enough," Randall said.

"Not as far as we're concerned," said one of the locals, "Are you OK, Brett?"

I just smiled. "Are we OK, Mr. Federal government man?"

Seeing he was badly outnumbered, he told me he just wanted to talk.

"Have a seat then. What can I do for you?"

Randall said, "I'm in charge of this operation."

"Really," I said, "What do you want with me?

"I need to know what happened at the farm and what part you played in it." Randall wanted the others at the table to leave.

I wasn't having that, and told Randall what he had witnessed at the Smith farm that first day. He left out the part about the hospital visit to Fred and Cassie, and the information Cassie had given them. He also left out the part where he and Helen went to the Smith farm and found the book in the basement.

And of course, I lied when asked about the video tape. He said he knew nothing about that.

"If you're lying to me, you're going to jail," Randall said.

"Good luck with that," I said, and then asked, "Have you killed her yet?"

"That's a matter of national security, and you're not on the need to know list." Randall looked around the room and then asked, "Who are these other people, and what are they doing here?"

"Just some friends of mine, here for a visit. What are you planning to do?" I asked.

It was Randall's turn to smile, "That's really none of your business," and with that Randall got up from the table, walked to the door, and turned around to face me, "We'll meet again, Deputy, and very soon." Randall and his crew walked out the door, and all the locals cheered and headed back to the farm.

Randall was pissed, nobody talked to him like that, and if he had more men, he would have arrested Brett--or at least tried to anyway. He was sure that Brett was holding out on him, he would have to send more men the next time he questioned him.

So far, it had been a quiet day at the farm, the demon and her little creatures just roamed around inside the fence. The men kept a close eye on them, and they kept their distance from the fence.

The demon knew they all were afraid of her, and she smiled at that. She wanted to wrap her hands around their necks and kill them all, "Soon," she thought, "very soon."

The demon had a plan. She wanted to trick Randall into releasing her, and then, in a few days, she wouldn't need him anymore.

Randall had decided on his way back to the farm that he didn't need the National Guard anymore, and so he ordered them to leave by tomorrow night. He didn't want any witnesses if things went bad. Some of his men voiced their objections to that decision. They thought the extra men would come in handy if it came to a showdown with the demon.

The demon was sure that even if that little white skinned man didn't free her, soon she would be strong enough to free herself. She longed to be free again, and didn't understand why her master couldn't free her. In fact, she'd no contact with him since she was trapped here.

It was a little after seven when the entire group hooked up at Happy Harry's, the plan was to get some food and head back to my place to go over all the information they had found today. Helen was very excited about Samuel's Bible and couldn't wait to go over all the information in it. Harry's was hopping tonight so they decided to stay awhile and do some serious drinking. Abraham not only liked to drink beer, he liked to sing as well, and it just so happened to be karaoke night at Harry's. Abraham sang a few of his favorite country songs. Helen and I spent a lot of time going over notes in Samuel's Bible and comparing them with what they already know. There had to be something there.

I said, "If she gets out, she's going to kill all of us. She might even go after the townspeople."

"We have to be prepared for that," Helen said. "There's a real good chance you're right about that."

They let the group have a little fun, and then headed over to Brett's to spend the night there.

The angel came to Abraham in his dreams for the first time that night. The angel told him to believe in his faith and that help would come when they needed it most. The angel told him that it was up to him to keep the group together at all costs, and that he couldn't tell the others about their conversation. He didn't understand, but agreed to be quiet about it.

Brett couldn't sleep, and decided to walk down to the shoreline. He loved the water, and it was peaceful and soothing sitting there on a downed tree at the water's edge. He could spend hours there looking out at the water. It was a perfect night for that with a full moon overhead. He was having a hard time understanding and believing all of this. What sane man would? If bullets couldn't stop her, what could? In the war, you just shot or dropped bombs on your enemy and that took care of them, but this... He shot her nine times, looking into her eyes, and it didn't faze her. Helen had told him that she believed the letters and symbols carved into the stone were holding the demon inside the fence. How do you turn letters and symbols into weapons and uses them against her? He thought they needed a weapon that didn't exist yet, and how could they know if she could be killed at all.

Helen and Abraham walked up behind him.

"We couldn't sleep, either," Abraham said, "mind if we join you?"

I told them, "There's plenty of room on this log, and it's a perfect place to think about what we're getting ourselves into. Can you tell me, truthfully, if you think we can we stop her if she gets out?"

Both of them shook their heads no. "Only God knows the answer to that," Abraham said.

Brett asked, "What are we doing here? I don't like fighting battles I can't win."

"We have to win this one, Brett. All the local people's lives are at stake.

"I understand that. What I don't understand is how we accomplish that."

Abraham had the answer. "We have to keep our faith in God's will, and I don't believe God wants this demon loose on earth."

"Great, just great," Brett said. "You know I've never been a true believer in all that religion stuff. I need more than just blind faith to go on."

"Then believe in us," Abraham said.

"I can do that. I can believe in all of you."

The demon was at her strongest this time of day. She was getting restless. She could almost taste her freedom. Yet, she could feel the presence of something from her past. She couldn't quite get a handle on it, and that bothered her. She went back to tormenting Randall's dreams. It was all too easy for her to manipulate him. Tonight she was going to set her children free for a while. She knew they couldn't stay outside the fence for very long, but she needed to send a message to the men guarding her. Her children wouldn't need to be out for very long to complete her task. They were getting restless, too. They also hungered to be free.

Randall was having a hard time sleeping again. He tried taking some sleeping pills, but they were having no effect on him. He got up and sat on the edge of his cot, going over the day's events. It didn't sound any better the second time around. He was even thinking of calling his superiors and asking for help. He knew if he did that, his career in government would be over, but he would rather have his career over then be dead. But in the end, Randall being Randall, he decided not to call them and would handle this the best way he could.

The three friends sat on that old tree for hours. When there was nothing left to talk about, about three in the morning, they walked back to Brett's cabin to try and get a few hours of sleep before dawn.

The swamp can be a very scary place at night. Unless there's a full moon, it's almost pitch black. Hiding in the shadows there are many things that can end a life in a heartbeat. The water is black and dirty, and the bugs… I think the bugs were the worst at night.

The guards were on edge tonight. Something was in the air. Something evil. The six guards were spaced an equal distance apart, even with all the lights, it was hard to see past the fence line. The shape of the fence meant that you could see only one of the other guards—maybe. They thought that with the motion detectors and sensors around the fence, they'd be safe.

The first of the guards went down around three a.m. No one noticed the little creatures as they climbed over the center of the fence between them. The little creatures seemed to be able to disappear at will. The guards didn't have a chance. Four of the creatures jumped on the first guard, and before he could shoot or signal the others, he was dead and laying on the ground. The creatures were told to kill three guards, and then hang them by their feet on the dead tree near the temple, inside the fence. She wanted to send a message to Randall, one that would get his attention. She had her creatures rip off the guards' heads before hanging them on the tree.

No one noticed the missing guards until morning, and the sensors hadn't gone off. How do you catch something that really wasn't there?

The demon knew that Randall got up at dawn and inspected the site as soon as the sun rose. She was hoping he would be the one to discover the bodies. She was planning on a big day; lots of things to screw with Randall's mind.

Lilith knew she would have to bring Gabriele back after the fence came down. She would force her to remove the spell. That damned old witch had been more trouble than she was worth. First things first, though, she needed to get that damned fence down, and then she would deal with Gabriele. It was just about dawn, and time to go her private world and rest a few hours. She smiled and wished she could see Randall's face in the morning when he saw the bodies in the trees. That should get his attention. She knew he was getting more paranoid as each day passed, and it would just be a matter of time until he was under her control.

───◦❊ **Day Four** ❊◦───

Randall was dreaming that he was back in grade school and the schoolyard bullies were picking on him again. Look at how small he is; he looks like he's in first grade not fifth grade, and they all laugh. His clothes look like hand me downs, and they laugh again, and this time the two biggest bullies kick him. He falls to the ground crying and hears them taunting him, "Look, the baby's crying. Must be time to change his diaper," and then they all run away laughing before they get caught. As he lays on the ground crying he hears a voice, "It's OK, Randall. I will help you, and someday, we can get even with those boys. We'll make them all pay. We'll hurt them in ways they can't imagine. All you have to do is free me. Take the fence down, and then it's you and me against them. Do you understand me, Randall?" And then, the voice starts laughing.

He woke up sweating and crying. He hated when people laughed at him. When he was young, it seemed that no matter what he did, people would pick on him and laugh at him. All he wanted was to fit in, to have friends; someone his own age that he could talk to and do things with. It was always the same. He was smaller than the other kids, and he was very shy and quiet. He was a perfect target for the bullies. They knew he wouldn't tell on them, and he was to small and weak to fight back. He'd been stuffed in so many lockers he'd lost count, but the worst was getting his head pushed into the toilet. He made sure to avoid the boys' bathrooms at all costs. It was about when he was in the eighth grade that he realized he was smarter than kids around him, so maybe he couldn't beat up the bullies, but he could out think them. From that point on, he spent all his time reading and studying. By the time he finished high school he was in the top three of his class, and in college he finished in the top five. During his last semester of college, he was approached by two men who said they worked for the government. They didn't come right out and say it, but Randall thought they were with the CIA. They told him that there was a new section of government that was just starting, and they wanted him to come and work for them. They said they had been watching him for a while, and liked his passion for the supernatural. It was a no brainer for Randall. He thought he was on his way. He thought somebody finally wanted and respected him, the real reason they wanted him was that they needed someone they thought they could control and manipulate. He was the right man for the job. It was too bad they didn't have faith in him, he was a very intelligent man with lots of potential. He just wasn't a very stable one. He would have flourished under the right set of circumstances, and just like when he was younger, he never had a chance.

Randall got up and realized he'd been crying in his sleep. He sat at the end of his bed thinking about how the demon had been getting into his dreams. He wondered how she knew about his childhood. Each of the last three nights his dreams had turned into nightmares; it was getting to the point that he was afraid to close his eyes anymore. If she would just let him sleep, he could think more clearly and make better decisions about the situation.

Just before dawn, Randall knew he was not going to be able to sleep anymore; she just wouldn't leave him alone. He left his tent and decided to take a look around the farm; he thought that would help him clear his mind. He walked back to the Smith farm house, and went inside. He thought that whoever lived here had a perfect life; living in the country, working the land, and taking care of livestock. He remembered thinking as a young kid that farming was a nothing job, and not very challenging. As he walked around inside the house, he looked at all the pictures hanging on the walls. There were many generations of Smith family pictures there. One caught his eye. It was an older picture of Sarah, Cassie and Jacob sitting on the front porch swing with Fred standing behind them. And by the boy's smile, you could tell that he was happy and loved by his parents. Randall envied them. He wondered why he couldn't have been born into a family like that, with a loving mother and father.

Randall wondered what had gone so wrong at the farm that changed it into what it is today. His compassion for other people had died long ago. Randall also wondered why the demon had come to the farm in the first place. What did she say? An angel and two religious men had tricked her. He didn't understand what she was talking about. He planned to ask her about that the next time he saw her. And he wondered who had helped these people build the fence and what short of spell it had that kept her trapped inside. It would appear that whoever built the fence and trapped the demon knew more about them than he did, and that bothered him. He came to the realization that knowing what the symbols meant was only half of the equation. He was sure that whoever carved the symbols in the stone also put a spell on them, and that there would never be a way to figure out what that was, so knowing what the symbols and letters meant likely wouldn't help him at all.

He walked upstairs and picked the bedroom at the end of the hallway. He didn't realize he had picked Jacob's old room. After his death, Fred didn't have the heart to enter his son's room again so he just shut the door and left it the way Jacob had left it the day he had died. Cassie went into the room once a week to keep things clean, but after her stroke she had a hard time keeping up with the cleaning, so for the last few years, the dirt and dust had started to collect there. He felt at peace there with all of Jacob's things scattered around the room. It was like he was a little boy again, and he didn't hear her voice in here. At first, he liked the feeling, but then all the bad things that had happened to him as a boy came back to him. He just couldn't catch a break.

Randall headed to the temple. He hoped that something positive would happen today. He knew he would try to question the demon today, and he hoped she would give him some of the answers he was looking for.

By now the National Guard was getting ready to leave and they should be gone by nightfall. That would mean that only his men were left guarding the temple. He ordered some heavy equipment to be brought up to the temple, including a backhoe and a bulldozer. His motto was hope for best, but be prepared for the worst—and he wanted to be prepared for worst. His men watched as the heavy equipment was brought to the temple. Randall thought they finally understood what he was planning to do, and none of them were too happy about it. They were talking among themselves, trying to come up with a plan to stop Randall, if it came to that.

Randall had hoped he could talk her into coming back with him to help him understand her powers. He thought he could control her and her powers. Now, though, he suspected that he had underestimated her strength and had to come up with a plan to capture her and take her back by force. And last, but not least, he had decided that if he couldn't control her, he would crush her and tear down the fence and the temple. By the time he was done there would no trace of her or this place left.

That would be his backup plan. If he had to, he could lie his way out of this with his superiors. It wouldn't be the first time he'd done that.

When he reached the fence, he noticed that the men were very jumpy. There was a small group of his men standing by the metal gate. It had been a long night for them too; sometime during the night three more men were killed and hung from trees by their feet. They couldn't figure out how anything could get past the fence line, the guards and the sensors.

Randall stood outside the fence staring at the dead, headless bodies hanging from the tree. This is a warning to me to release her, he thought to himself. He pictured himself hanging from the tree. He wondered if the men were alive when she tore their heads off. He could almost feel his head being pulled off. He had to physically shake those thoughts out of his mind, and get back to work.

Randall felt as if, somehow, things had changed overnight. He could feel it in the air, and it wasn't a good. Something had the ability to get outside the fence, and that was freaking out all the men. They couldn't fight what they couldn't see or hear, and whatever it was had even gotten past the motion detectors. He now knew no one was safe. He decided to bring in an advisor, a priest, from the main office. Randall knew the priest had drinking and money problems that had lost him his church. It seemed that the priest's brother-in-law, a high ranking government official, helped him get hired in the new division the government was forming. It made sense to have a religious man on staff when they were studying the occult. When Randall called and asked him to come to the farm to help, he said he was too busy and couldn't take the time. Randall was ready for his excuse, and told him if he didn't come, he would tell his brother-in-law he was drinking again and get him fired. The priest was backed into a corner and said he would be there in the morning. Randall didn't like blackmailing him, but he had no choice. He didn't know if the priest would be any help, but he thought he couldn't hurt.

Randall knew he had a few hours to get some things done inside the fenced area before the demon and her children appeared. The men didn't want to enter the fenced area until Randall explained to them that it should be safe to enter for a few hours.

When the demon appeared, she spent most of her time floating around the fence line, staring at the men. There always seemed to be several little creatures that followed the demon around inside fenced area. Children. That's what she called them—her children. They didn't look like children, and he wondered what they really were. Whatever they were, they were deadly, and very loyal to her. Once the sun came up things seemed quieter, and there was no sign of them at all.

Randall sent his men inside the fenced area a little after sunrise to remove the dead from the tree, and to check out the area and the temple for anything that could help him. Once inside, they set up more of their sensors and cameras, they videotaped the interior of the temple, took dirt samples from the floor, and then installed more cameras and sensors inside the small room. They even set a few booby traps around the outside of the fence. They doubted they would hurt the creatures, but at least it would give the men a little warning that they were outside the fence.

Now it was a waiting game. The men reinforced their positions around the outside of the fence. They built bunkers about fifty feet apart and had big machines guns installed in each one. The area was looking more like a battle zone then a cemetery. The men hooked the chain around the metal gate again, and then retreated to the safety of the perimeter.

The dirt samples came back negative. It was just dirt. And the central office sent a message saying that the markings on the stone columns and door were an unknown language. His research team couldn't find any more information on Samuel Stone or Eagle Claw, maybe it was just a coincidence that the two men had died there and were buried by the fence line. Who the hell knew any more.

Randall's superiors had called again. They were getting concerned about the mission, and with the latest loss of life, they were thinking of moving up his timetable. They were at a point where they didn't believe a word that Randall was telling them. They didn't believe that there was a demon trapped inside the fence. He chose not to take their call, and instead, sent them a message that he would call them later. He had no intension of calling them back until his mission was finished. His superiors figured it would take at least two days to get another team leader up to speed, head out to the farm site, and take over the operation from Randall. One way or another, Randall would be relieved by the end of the week.

Helen and I got up early and headed over to Harry's for breakfast. They let the others sleep in. There were going to be a few hangovers this morning, so the extra sleep would do them good. They left a note telling the others to meet them at the roadhouse around lunch time.

Even though they were getting a lot of answers about the demon, a big one remained unanswered: how to stop her. They went over everything that had happened from day one while they ate their breakfast.

Helen had Brett repeat the story of the first day to see if she had missed anything, and then day two and three. There just wasn't anything there to help them. At about nine o'clock, they decided to take a break and head over to the hospital to see how Fred and Cassie were doing.

They were surprised that the guards were all gone. They were told that Randall had called them back to the farm late last night. Hospital staff were really glad to see them go. The doctors told them that Fred was doing much better today, and that they were hoping that he would come out of his coma in the next few days. They said that they expected him to make a full recovery.

The lady from the ghost hunter's show was a different matter. It seemed that she had a complete mental breakdown. She was heavily medicated. The doctors thought she would never be the same and were making plans to send her to a place that was better suited to help people in her condition.

Cassie was about the same. She was getting restless and wanted to go home. The hospital wasn't going to release her unless there was going to be someone else at the farm to watch over her, and so far, no one had volunteered for the job. She was probably going to have to stay in the hospital till Fred got out.

When they entered her room, she smiled and started writing on her notepad. She asked if the two had found the book. They told her that they had and that they had found Abraham in Chicago and brought him back to Church Point. Cassie had never met Abraham, but she knew he was an old family friend who had saved Fred's life all those years ago. Cassie asked about the demon, and Helen told her things were getting tense, but that the demon was still trapped behind the fence. She told Cassie that they were afraid that Randall would do something stupid and release her. They also told her they didn't have any idea how to stop the demon if she got out. Helen asked if Cassie had any ideas on how to stop her.

Cassie explained in a note that she had never seen the demon. She said that when she first arrived at the farm, Fred told her about the legend and let her read the book. She said that at first, she didn't know what to believe, but felt better when they told her the demon hadn't been seen for over sixty years—and she made it a point to stay the hell away from temple. Cassie wrote that she had no idea how to stop her.

She asked if they would pray with her, and she grabbed each of their hands. She wrote another note and told them that no matter what keep they needed to keep their faith and that God would come through for them.

Cassie was a deeply religious woman. It was her faith that helped her through the trying times after her daughter died. She pulled the necklace she was wearing off and gave it to Helen. She wrote that it was her daughter's and that she wanted to give it to her for luck.

Helen didn't want to accept it, but when she saw the look in Cassie's eye's, she changed her mind. She put the necklace on, bent over, and gave Cassie a kiss on her cheek. They told her they would check on her in a day or two.

She had a sad smile on her face, and knew in her heart that she would never see them again. She had grown quite found of these two people. When they left, she moved her wheelchair over to the window and watched them get in their car and drive away. She silently said another prayer for them. Cassie didn't know if she would ever see Fred again, either, and she wanted to say a few last things to him. She started writing a letter to him, telling him how much she loved him, what a good husband and father he was to her daughter and grandson, and how thankful she had been to him for letting her live with him all these years. She told him it was the happiest time of her life. She wrote that she felt her time was coming to an end, and that she would soon be joining her daughter and grandson. She would miss him and the farm.

It's funny how some people know when death is coming. I don't know if it's a blessing or a curse, but she had lived a long and good life, and if this was her time, she could accept it.

About the middle of the afternoon things started changing at the temple. The red mist started forming, and the little creatures started appearing. Every day there was more and more mist, and it was getting darker in color. So far, they hadn't been able to get samples of it. Every time they tried, the mist just disappeared. It seemed that the mist was almost a living thing. It was just another reason for Randall and his men to finish this and leave.

As the demon made her first appearance of the day, the sky became overcast and it looked as if it might rain, and it always seemed that the center of the storm was over the Smith farm. Randall saw her standing by the temple with the creatures at her feet. They seemed to follow her everywhere. Today there were several taller looking creatures, almost the size and shape of a man. They were very scary looking things. They had a vacant look in their eyes. Randall wondered if they were her children too. If they attacked, they would be a handful to contend with. The smaller creatures were bad enough.

Randall's men knew something was about to happen so they got their weapons out, entered their bunkers, and waited. She came to the fence and stared at Randall. He seemed hypnotized by her. He didn't realize it, but she was feeding off his fear, and his men's fear as well. She asked Randall how he liked the present she left for him last night, and then asked when he was going to free her.

"It depends on you," he said, "I need you to cooperate with us. We need to study you, and learn how you do the things you do. We need to know what kind of power holds you to this place, and what all those symbols mean. I need to know why you came here, and most of all, I need to know what you are and what you could do for me if I free you."

She smiled and said, "You ask a lot little man. I'll tell you what. If you free me right now, I will let you and your men live. That's my deal. Soon I will be strong enough, and I won't need you."

He needed to make up his mind soon. She was mocking him and laughing at him. For the first time since this started, he became really scared of her and this place.

She told him that the two graves at the outside of the fence contained the remains of the men who had trapped her, and then she said, "We can always add a third grave for you, if you don't release me. What do you think about that Randall?"

This wasn't the answer he was expecting, and he slowly backed away from the fence—keeping his eyes on her as he did.

It was then that she had the larger creatures destroy all the sensors and cameras inside the fence. Once that was finished, the larger creatures rushed the gate and broke the chain holding it in place. The gate swung open and they stormed out. The red mist followed them through the opening and past the fence line, and then the creatures started attacking and killing his men. All of their weapons were useless against them. One by one, the men started going down. After a few minutes, the creatures made their way back into the temple area carrying all sorts of body parts with them. The red mist followed them back inside. It was clear now that only she was trapped behind the fence. So now he knew that the creatures got out of the fenced area and killed his men last night.

Randall was terrified as he watched the creatures kill his men. He thought it was strange that the creatures stayed away from him, and just attacked his men. He looked for and found her. She was floating about twenty feet above the ground, laughing. "I'm saving you for last Randall. You're going to watch as all your men are killed."

She had spread her arms, and as soon as all of her children were back inside the fence, she started laughing.

He didn't understand. She had just killed nearly half of his men and she was laughing about it. Why didn't she just finish killing everybody? Then it hit him. If she killed everybody, there would be no one left to tear down the fence and set her free. He wanted this all to end. As he looked around at all the bodies of his men, he became physically sick. The remaining men had to help him back to his sleeping quarters. They were powerless against her and the creatures. The ones who were left had seen enough, and wanted to leave. A few of the battle hardened ones started to put what remained of the dead soldiers into body bags.

After the attack, most of her children either faded into the red mist or wandered into the temple and disappeared. The demon smiled at him, and asked, "Have you had enough Randall? Are you ready to free me now?" she asked.

"Why are you doing this?" he asked.

"You know the answer to that, Randall. You have been brought here to free me, and if I have to kill a few people for you to see the light, so be it."

"You didn't have to kill them."

"But I like killing people, Randall, and I'm really good at it, don't you think?" Then she started laughing.

God, how he hated being laughed at. Things were really getting out of control, and Randall was having second thoughts about trying to capture her. He knew, at this point, it would never happen. He just didn't know what to do.

The second layer of defense, the National Guard, heard the screaming and gunfire and moved further back they couldn't leave this place fast enough. They had been ordered to leave, and that's what they were going to do. They really didn't know what was happening here, and Randall had pissed them off so badly they didn't care.

He ordered the earth moving equipment up and was going to start tearing down the fence and the temple. He thought if it come to that, he could crush her and her creatures. The men spent the rest of the afternoon putting the dead into body bags and getting them ready to be taken back home for burial. Randall was worried about calling his superiors. If they found out there was more loss of life, they would pull the plug on this operation and replace him. He couldn't have that, so he decided to wait till morning to call them. That should give him enough time to try and put a spin on what's happening here.

Randall had one more shot; the priest he had sent for should be here in the morning. He had nothing left to lose, and if he couldn't help, he had decided he was going to knock down the fence and release her. Randall's men had lost all their faith in his ability to lead. They all thought he was just a step away from insanity.

His second in command had been in contact with Randall's superiors and informed them what was really happening here. They were told that under no circumstances were they to tear down the fence. If they had to, they were ordered to shoot him. They were sending a new team to take over the operation that should be there in two days. Their new orders were to contain the area and prevent further loss of life. They knew the new orders weren't going to go over well with Randall, so they decided to play it cool until Randall forced their hand. All they had to do was keep Randall from tearing down the fence till reinforcements got there. That shouldn't be too hard to do.

On the drive over from the hospital, Helen asked Brett if he thought Cassie was acting a little strange today.

He said, "I thought she was a little off, but you have to remember what's she's been through the last few days. The first time I saw Cassie, I was afraid of her. And now, getting to know her, my opinion has changed. I enjoyed spending time with her, though she still scares me a little."

Helen said, "She reminds me of my mother, tough, strong and yet a very caring person."

Helen and I pulled into the parking lot at Harry's at the same time as the others. After some teasing about last night's activities, they headed inside and sat around the large conference table at the back of the bar. They went over everything, and the research team told them they thought the demon's name was Lilith.

"If that's true," said Helen, "we're all in trouble. According to legend, Lilith was one of the first demons to walk the earth. She was the first women demon, and many considered her to be the daughter of the devil. She is a very old and a very powerful demon that has more powers then the run of the mill demon."

The research team also knew why the demon had been summoned, but didn't know why this particular one came, and why she didn't leave after she killed all the soldiers four hundred years ago.

Helen told them that when an event like the massacre happened it left a presence, or energy, that got absorbed into the land. "All of us have had that feeling before when you walk into a room and you get goosebumps and your heart rate begins to soar. Sometimes, the energy of the presence is so strong it could last forever, and perhaps, somehow, the demon is tied to this place because of that presence. Maybe we should just ask her."

The others in the group didn't think that was funny.

Abraham mentioned that as a young child he was told stories about the swamp. In those stories, there was a battle between good and evil before man's time on earth. Evil lost and was banished into the swamp for all time. There was another old story that the natives of the area believed the swamps were the passage to heaven, and evil was here trying to stop people from getting there.

Helen said, "That makes sense. There are areas all over the world that are just plain evil. Call them what you want, there are places where the hair on the back of your neck stands up when you enter the area. We've all had that feeling at one point of our lives. Maybe Brett was right, and the Smiths were just very unlucky and picked the cursed land to settle on. But if the land was so evil, why would the natives consider it to be sacred land?"

Nothing was making any sense to them. Everybody was just guessing why the demon came, and why it stayed it really didn't matter. All that mattered was how to get rid of it.

After four days of this, it was finally sinking in that we were talking about demons and witches like it was an everyday thing.

Somehow, this didn't feel real. I half expected to wake up and find that this was just a dream, but I was there and saw the demon with my own eyes. I saw her kill two of my friends. This was no dream. It was a nightmare—and one that didn't seem to ever go away.

After spending most of the afternoon and evening going over options, we figured it would be safer if we went out to the Smith farm in the morning. If the government wasn't involved, the best decision would have been to let sleeping dogs sleep, but it was too late for that now. There was going to have to be some sort of resolution at the farm, one way or another.

We decided to have supper at Harry's, It had been our home away from home for the last few days, and it felt like this was going to be our last meal. I was glad there was a band playing. It would help lighten the mood and take our minds off of what would happen in the morning.

Abraham was enjoying his beer again when a friend of mine came up and told the group that he had heard the National Guard was leaving the Smith farm by tonight. He said that the Fed's had told everyone that they had it under control and it would be over in a couple of days. The Fed's had already started their damage control, and had spread rumors about a group of home grown crazies who had gotten ahold of some chemical weapons and were hiding in the swamp at the Smith farm when the TV crew had stumbled on to them by mistake. The story went that there was a shootout and the crew was killed, along with some local boys from the sheriff's department and highway patrol. It was a hell of a story, and to be honest, it was more believable than the truth.

I could see the general public buying it, and at this point, I just didn't care. I just wanted to put an end to the demon and move on.

My friend started to ask questions about what I knew, and he said that a lot of the locals were concerned about what was happening out there. They didn't really believe the stories that the government was passing around, and a few of them wanted to head out to the farm to check it out for themselves. I told him I was going out there tomorrow to check it out and asked them to be patient for a day or two, and that I'd let them know what was going on. They wanted to go with, but I talked them out of it. I was worried that they'd confront Randall and his men, and it just wouldn't be the right time for that to happen.

I had a very bad feeling that Randall was going to do something very dumb, and that it would affect everybody in the area.

Back at the farm, Randall was glad he had decided to send the National Guard home. He didn't want anybody to see his failure, and up until now, they hadn't really seen anything. Sure, they heard the screams and the gunfire, but they were so far back and were well hidden from what was happening that there was no way for them to know for sure. Randall's men watched as the last truck left the farm, and to a man, they thought it was a huge mistake to let them go. They knew if she got out they would need all the firepower they could get their hands on. After watching them leave, the men turned around and headed down the dirt path toward the temple as the sun was setting. Many of them knew the end would be coming soon.

Randall had made up his mind that if the priest couldn't destroy her in the morning, he would tear down that damned fence and set her free. He just couldn't take any more of this place and that demon. He thought if she was free she would leave and go back to wherever she had come from. He liked his new plan. It wasn't the best solution, but he was running out of options and time. Just maybe, he could pull it off and keep his job. In his mind, he thought he'd have everything done before his supervisors' visit. He'd have everything done just in the nick of time. He would finish this by tomorrow and have it all cleaned up by the time they got here. They just had to make it through one more night.

He couldn't get her voice out of his head. It was ringing in his hears. It just wouldn't stop. First the dammed dreams, and now that voice. He wished she would just shut up and leave him alone.

Randall and his men pulled back to the safety of the old farm house for the night. He was dreading sleep. Since the sleeping pills didn't help, he decided to go the other way. He drank every energy drink he could get his hands on. He was wired. His men thought he'd have a heart attack from the stuff. He drifted in and out of sleep that night. At one point, he was wide awake and in a sweat. He kept thinking his plan sounded great, but he wondered about the cost and whether he could trust her to keep her word. He wished she would just let him sleep. He was so very tired.

His first in command was keeping a close eye on him. When he had contacted Randall's superiors and informed them that the situation at the farm was getting worse they told him to watch Randall very carefully, and not to let him do anything that would lead to more people being killed. Randall wouldn't be happy about that, but they were way past caring about his feelings now.

Brett was getting a little drunk, and he wasn't the only one. He noticed that for an old man Abraham could really throw them down, and the researchers could hold their own too. They even danced. He wondered if this is what men did the night before a battle, knowing there was a good chance that most of them would die tomorrow. Maybe knowing you might die in the morning makes you appreciate the things you have, and enjoy them a little more. He pushed those thoughts from his mind and tried to enjoy the time he had left with his new found friends.

The energy drinks had finally worn off, and Randall drifted off to sleep. He felt so very relaxed. It was the best sleep he had in days.

He felt something tugging on his arm and he opened his eyes. He was deep inside the fenced area, and standing right in front him was the demon, surrounded by her children. He was terrified.

She stepped closer until she was face to face with him. She looked into his eyes.

He couldn't look at her so just stared at the ground. His men were outside the fence watching him. Somehow, he had gotten up and sleepwalked to the temple, opened the gate, and walked inside.

"Look at me," the demon said. "Randall, did you have a nice nap? You're going to have a big day tomorrow. Perhaps you should return to the farm house for the rest of the night, but if you prefer, you could spend the night in the temple with us. It's your choice, and Randall, remember this… that you are the only man who has walked out of here alive in over two hundred years. So have a nice night. I will see you tomorrow." She started to laugh as he slowly walked backwards through the gate and returned to the farmhouse.

He didn't sleep the rest of the night. He kept thinking of her standing right in front of him, with no fence between them He could feel how truly evil she was, and he could sense that her little creatures wanted to tear him apart, but were holding back until she gave the word.

Her control over him was now almost complete. He could feel himself slipping away, and he was utterly terrified about that. Why she didn't kill him just didn't make sense to him anymore, and then there was the look on the faces of his men. He knew no one trusted him now. His world was collapsing around him. There was no way out. There was no fixing this.

He knew he had come to the right decision about tearing down the fence. He only hoped that she would keep her word and leave once she was free.

It was well past midnight when Brett and his crew left Harry's, and none of them were feeling any pain. Brett had seen a lot of death in the war. He knew that when your time came, there would be no stopping it. That was when the people alongside you became your family, and that was all that mattered; having someone that cares for you, standing by you at the end. Brett was glad they had tonight. It would be something that they would cherish for a long time.

Lilith watched the men head back to their tent city. She was floating about twenty feet in the air as they left. Things were going well. She thought that perhaps in two days at the most, she would be free.

She was enjoying thinking about what to do with Randall. At first, she thought she would make him her slave, like she had with all the others, but he wasn't like the others. So she thought she would make his death a very painful and very slow one. She smiled at the thought of that. Her mind drifted back to a time when she was free to roam the earth. She had enjoyed causing pain and suffering, and she had done a lot of that with her time here on earth. She could hardly wait to continue on her path.

Just then she trembled. She looked around anxiously. She had that feeling again. She knew the angels were close. She wished they would just show themselves. She knew she could handle one by herself, and she had her children to help if there were other angels.

She smiled and thought of her children. They were actually humans whom she had killed and brought back with the red mist to serve her. The old witch Gabriele was pissed when she found out what she had done to her people. The only one I couldn't turn was that dammed old witch. "As soon as I'm free, I'm going to bring her back and have her lift the curse she placed on me and the land, and then I'm going to send her to the afterlife where she belongs."

She was worried about those angels. She would have to stay on her toes. She couldn't afford to get trapped again. The master wouldn't be pleased if I couldn't get free this time. Everything was riding on that weak little man, Randall. She could sense that he was close to his breaking point. One more day. Just one more day, and he would do anything she asked.

The demon was right about the angels. They were watching—and waiting—as the game played out on the little farm in Louisiana. They were also waiting to see what Randall would do. To them, it was just a matter of waiting till the time was right to strike.

Day Five

After leaving the fenced area, Randall was having trouble walking, and barley made it back to the Smith farm house. He looked at his watch; a little past three a.m. He was still shaking from having come face to face with the demon. He sat on the edge of the bed thinking that it had turned out to be a very bad day for him.

More of his men had been killed, and he was sure that the men who were left were turning against him. And then, there was that dammed demon. It finally came to him that she couldn't be defeated. It defied everything that he believed in. There were no books or protocol on what to do next. How do you defeat an undefeatable evil? He knew he was in trouble, and he was desperate now.

All Randall's hopes rested on the priest now, but the priest had been a little reluctant to come to the Smith farm after Randall told him what he needed help with. He had given in against his better judgment, and told Randall he would be there before nine o'clock the next day. The priest didn't know a lot about the supernatural, just the few things they taught him at school and the movies he had watched. He was pushed into religion by his father and his faith wasn't where it should be. It had been severely tested by his drinking problem.

Randall had him by the balls, the priest's brother-in-law had warned him there would be no more chances, and that if he was caught drinking again he would be fired, family or not. Randall had caught him drinking in his office late one night when everyone else had gone home. The priest had begged him not to tell anyone, he told Randall he would do anything to keep it between the two of them. That went straight to Randall's head. For the first time in his life, he felt powerful and agreed to keep it a secret, on condition that the priest owed him a favor down the road. The favor was now due.

After tossing and turning for a few hours, Randall went outside and sat on the porch swing, the same swing that he had seen in the picture with that young family. He kept looking down the dirt road that led to the temple, and wondering how it had come to this. He could hear the demon and her children screaming, nobody could understand what they were saying. They seemed to be screaming just for the sake of screaming. It was getting on everybody's nerves.

The sky above the temple had taken on a dark red color with streaks of black running through it. He had never seen a night sky that color before, and wondered if that was a sign of things to come.

He was a broken man. He knew he couldn't make it through another night of this. He watched the sun come up over the farm as he reflected on his life. Sitting there he finally realized that most of things that had happened to him in his life were out of his control, just like what was happening at the farm. He would need to find a way through this, a way to survive. It looked like it was going to be a clear warm day. He got off the swing and walked down the dirt path toward the temple. For the first time since this started, he felt calm and in control, or maybe he felt relieved, that after today he wouldn't have to deal with the demon anymore. He could get on with his life. He was going to end this nightmare today one way or another.

A few of Randall's men had taken off during the night. They had had enough. The few men who had stayed were worried that Randall was going to free her, and they were convinced that if he did, they were all going to die.

Randall tried calming their fears by telling them that she could have killed him last night, and she hadn't, so that proved to him that she would keep her word and leave if she was set free. He told them about the priest coming this morning, and tried to convince the men that things would turn in the right direction once he got here. He did his best sales job, and said that if the priest failed, they would tear down the fence and release her.

No one believed what he had said about the priest, but it bought the men a little more time. All they needed was a couple of more days for the replacements to arrive. Once they got here, Randall would be their problem. The men were prepared to kill him if they had too.

She seemed to have almost unlimited powers, and once she was free, there was no telling what she would do.

His men would have to be very cautious over the next day or two if they wanted to survive this, and that's all they were thinking about now; surviving.

Randall's superiors had tried to call him that morning. He ignored their calls. The demon seemed to know that they were trying to reach Randall's men, and sent one of her children to deal with it. The radio operator had his back to the tent door when the creature entered the tent. He was completely invisible and slipped right through all the men without being seen. The creature stood behind the soldier watching him, they liked watching the humans. The creature waited till the phone started ringing and then jumped on the soldier's back, wrapped his hands around the man's head, and drove his fingers into the man's eyes, killing him instantly. The man's body started quivering, and the creature held on to it until it stopped. He released the dead man and let the body drop to the ground. The creature had one more task to complete before he could return to the temple. He dug a small hole in the dirt floor in the middle of the tent, and then watched as the red mist rose out of it. The mist engulfed the radio equipment and destroyed it. As the mist slowly sank back into the ground, the little creature became invisible again and made his way back to the temple.

The bitter smell that had hung in the air the last few mornings seemed to be worse today. The guards who were ex-soldiers knew the smell. It was the smell of death; burning, rotting, human flesh. Several of the men got sick from the smell. The smell seemed to be centered on the temple, so to get any relief from the stink, you had to walk down the dirt path away from the temple toward the Smith farmhouse.

All the dead bodies had disappeared during the night; every last body bag had been taken. No one saw or heard anything. Nothing that was happening here surprised the men anymore. They had seen enough unexplainable events to last a lifetime. The only things on their minds that morning were thoughts about staying alive, and most of them figured that wasn't going to happen.

They would all die in this stinking swamp.

Besides the smell, the temple and surrounding area had taken on a darker look. The darkness was spreading out from the center of the temple and was sucking all the life out of the area. Any wildlife in the area had vanished overnight; even the animals knew death was coming and moved as far away from this place as they could.

Back at the Brett's place Helen was trying to convince her team to head back home; it would be much safer she told them. They refused.

She reluctantly agreed, but told them this would be their last day here and that in the morning they were going home, no matter what happened today, and that if anyone got hurt this morning, they would all need to leave as fast as possible.

After breakfast as the group was getting ready to head back to the farm, Abraham, being the old preacher he was, gathered them in a circle and said a few prayers. Then they were off, not knowing what the day would bring or if they'd be alive at the end of the day.

Randall had instructed his men to bring the backhoe the first thing this morning. He wanted to be ready to tear down the fence if he had to. His men tried one last time to tell him to chain up the gate and leave her behind the fence.

His first in command knew the replacements wouldn't arrive till tomorrow afternoon, and he stalled for time. If he had to, he would shoot Randall to stop him.

Randall was worried about his men. He knew he couldn't trust them anymore and he didn't like the way they were looking at him. It bothered him that they always stopped talking when he was around.

He could sense their fear, and he didn't know who to fear more—his men or the demon. He looked at the faces of his men and saw doubt in their eyes. He would have to be very careful from here on out. It all came down to this. He was determined to see his plan through no matter what his men thought. Randall didn't usually carry a sidearm, but after looking at his men, he decided that he would start wearing one today. He wanted to be prepared if it came to that.

It was about a thirty minute drive to the Smith farm from Brett's house.

There had been very little talking on the drive over. He had asked if anyone had any ideas at all about how to deal with the demon. They all just looked at each other and said no.

As they pulled into the Smith driveway, he was surprised that the guardsmen were all gone. He thought they would have left a small group of soldiers to keep an eye on things. "This can't be good," he told Helen.

The farm site was a mess. It almost looked as if there had been a rock concert there, and Fred would be pissed when he got back.

It was a dark overcast day, and no one had seen them yet. That was when they noticed the smell. Brett knew what it was. He had smelled it many times when he was overseas. The others didn't quite know what to make of it, and a couple of them got sick.

Helen told her team to stay by the house and be ready to leave at a moment's notice; that if they heard any gunfire or screaming, they were to get in their cars, leave this place, and head back to the university. She looked one last time at her friends, and then she, Brett and Abraham walked down the dirt road toward the temple.

Randall watched the three come up the road and head toward him. He signaled his men to let them through. "So you decided to come back. How nice of you," he said. "I should shoot you all for your part in this. You have caused me nothing but grief since I got here. Speak your peace, and then leave and let me and my men do our jobs."

"We're only here to help you try and end this," Brett said.

"Who the hell do you think you are? What makes you think we need your help?"

"Do you and your men really know what you're facing?" Helen asked.

"Yes, I do. And it's a matter of national security—and way above your pay grade."

I turned to Randall, "Why don't you save your bullshit for someone that doesn't know any better. We're in the middle of a swamp facing a creature that has been trapped for hundreds of years. She's a demon that has powers beyond your comprehension. If you make the wrong move, she will not only kill you and your men, she could turn on the town. If she gets out, there's no stopping her."

"I have my orders, and they are to either capture her or kill her. There is no in-between, and that's what I intend to do."

Helen said, "That's easier said than done. Just how do you intend to do that?"

One thing that Randall hated was being questioned by people whom he thought were beneath him. "That's government business, and how I proceed is my choice—not yours."

Randall's men had gathered around them.

"Let them speak. We want to hear what they have to say. Let us help you," Abraham said. "We're on your side. We only want to see this thing end with everybody still alive.

Brett joined the argument, "Helen is one of the world's top research scientists in the field of the supernatural, and Abraham faced the demon sixty years ago as a young boy. The three of us know more about what's happening here than anybody else. You have to let us help you."

"I have my orders, and I intend to carry them out."

"All we're asking is that you take a little more time and make sure you get it done right the first time," Brett said.

"We don't have any more time, she said she would be strong enough in a day or two to break through the fence by herself, and then we'd lose all control."

"And you believe her?" Helen asked. "Why you don't ask Abraham about how good her word is. She's been trapped behind that fence for over a hundred and fifty years, don't you think if she had been able to free herself she would done that a long time ago?"

"That doesn't matter. She's getting stronger every day, and I believe her." As the group argued, the priest arrived. He drove down the dirt path and stopped as he came into the clearing where everyone was standing and talking.

Randall saw the priest and told the others that help was there.

The tall skinny priest got out of his car and walked toward the group with a Bible in his hand.

"It's about time you showed up," Randall scolded.

"I got lost on the way here from Church Point."

"That doesn't matter, as long as you're here now." Randall filled Father Paul in on what had been happening and what he thought they were facing; the short version of it anyway. He didn't want to scare the priest away with the truth.

Paul really didn't believe any of this, but had no choice. He thought he could say a few verses from the Bible and sprinkle a little holy water on the ground to make everybody happy, and then head home.

Brett looked over at Paul and said, "You're kidding me. What do you think he can do against her?"

"He's a holy man, and I trust him," Randall said. "It's good against evil, and all that bullshit. He's going to help us capture her and keep her under control so she doesn't hurt any more people. And then, he's going to accompany her back to headquarters where we can learn what she really is, and how her powers work."

"And how's he going to do that?" Abraham asked.

"By my faith in God and the holy Bible," Paul said. "God is the creator of the universe and all powerful."

Abraham shook his head, and said, "You're making a big mistake."

Father Paul frowned, and said, "Just stay out of my way and let me do my work." He walked to the front of the fence gate, opened his Bible, and started reading from it. As he did, red mist started coming up from ground inside the fenced area. Something looked different today.

"The mist never showed up this early before," Randall said, "and it's darker than before."

Brett ran to the fence gate, shoved it shut, and wrapped the chain around it. With the gate closed and locked he thought they would have some protection against the demon and her children.

Randall looked at Brett and said, "Those little creatures aren't bound by the fence. They can climb over it any time they want. The demon is the only one that can't cross the fence line." He tried pulling the priest away from the fence, but Father Paul just shook him off and said, "I'm a man of God, and I fear no evil."

Brett backed away to rejoin his small group.

"Very clever," came a voice from inside the temple, "but it's too late for that now. It won't help you or stop me."

All eyes turned toward the woman floating toward them from the temple with all of her little children following her.

Paul noticed her and the creatures for the first time, and slowly backed away from the fence. He stepped behind the others, not believing what he was seeing.

She walked right up to the fence and said, "It's time to decide. Are you ready to set me free, Randall?"

He was trapped, and didn't know what to do. He wavered, and then said, "If I set you free, will you leave and not hurt any more people?"

She smiled. "Of course. I just want to be free. You have my word on it. As soon as you free me, I will leave this place forever, and you will never see me again." That was then she saw the other people. "Abraham, I see you came back. How nice to see you again. Your father says hello. Have you come to join him?" She laughed.

Abraham walked up to the fence, looked her in the eye, and said, "I have come back to send you back to hell."

She stopped laughing. "Give it your best shot, Old Man. Better men than you have tried, and all have failed."

She looked at Helen and said, "I know you. You think that you're so smart. When I'm free, I'm going to show you how little you know about me and my kind. You're all fools, and the longer you keep me here, the harder it's going to be on you."

Her eye's caught sight of Paul who had moved away from the fence and was standing behind the group. All his color was gone, and he stood there shaking. "Who do we have here? Another religious man?"

Paul, who started to back away from her said, "You can't be real."

She laughed and said, "I see you're a true believer. This will be fun."

All at once, he started floating toward the fence. Before the others could react, he floated up and over the fence. On the other side, the demon's children became visible and carried him to her feet. He lay crying as she said, "Stand up and face me if you want to live."

He did as he was told and slowly got to his feet.

"How are you going to stop me, Priest?"

He opened his Bible and started reading from it. He pulled the holy water out of his pocket and splashed some on her.

She looked at Randall and said, "Really? Is this your best attempt to stop me?" She started laughing. "Let me show you what happens to non-believers. You will see what real power is."

Paul seemed to float off the ground again, till he was about ten feet up. He was turned to face the others who were outside the fence. His arms raised up till he formed the shape of a cross with his body. He was flipped upside down with all her children forming a circle around him. The demon stood in front of him and asked, "Do you believe in God?"

"What?" he asked.

"It's an easy question. Do you really believe in God?"

"Of course I do."

"Do you think he will save you?" she asked.

"He will save my soul."

"We will see about that," and all at once he burst into flames.

All that the others could do was watch in horror as he screamed and burned to death.

After he stopped screaming, she turned to the others and saw the fear in their eyes. With a sweeping motion of her hands, Paul's burning dead body flew over the fence at the group. They barely got out of the way as his burning body hit the ground.

She looked at the group and asked, "Do you think his God saved his soul?" She stared at Randall. "What's it going to be, life or death? If you don't let me go, Randall, I will haunt your dreams forever. You will never have a peaceful night's sleep again, and in the end, I will get out anyway."

Randall was terrified, and ordered his men to tear down the fence.

No one moved. The men weren't going to follow that order.

Brett seeing what Randall was going to do, asked him to give it more thought so that his group could come up with something to keep the demon trapped.

"Stay out of this," Lilith screamed at Brett. "This is between Randall and me.

"What's one more day?" Brett pleaded with Randall.

"No. She's right. It has to end today. What can you do, anyway? We've tried everything to stop her. There is no other way. We have to tear down the fence and release her. You heard her, she said she would leave and not hurt anyone else."

Abraham said, "You can't trust her. If you let her out, she will kill all of us, and then turn on the town. Do you know who this demon is Randall?"

"Of course, I do. It's Lilith.

Abraham went on, "If you know her name, you know what's she's capable of, and the powers she has."

"That doesn't change a thing. She promised to leave and not hurt any more people."

Brett stepped closer, and into the argument. "Do you really believe her? She will kill you and your men the first chance she gets."

Helen grabbed Brett by the arm and told him, "We're wasting our time with him. We need to get out of here. He's not going to listen. We can't be here if she gets out." The three turned and ran back toward the house.

Randall yelled at his men, "If you don't tear the fence down, I will."

His men blocked his way, and that's when he pulled his gun and shot two of them; one, his first in command. Some of the men ran toward the farm house, while others backed away. "You can run all you want she will find you wherever you go. There is no hiding from her." And with that, Randall got in the backhoe and started toward the fence.

Brett, Helen and Abraham had reached the car and were yelling for the others to get in and get the hell out of there. No one was going to argue. In minutes, they were driving down the road and away from the farm.

Once Randall had reached the fence with the backhoe, he stopped the backhoe and sat quietly watching the demon. He wanted to make sure she was going to keep her promise and not hurt him or the men.

She was floating a few feet above the ground, staring at him. Such a weak little man, she thought to herself. "Why have you stopped?" she asked.

"I'm not sure this is the right thing to do," he said.

"You have no choice, but to finish what you've started," she said. "No harm will come to you or your men. I promise you that."

He climbed back in and brought the arm of the backhoe down on the metal gate, tearing it away from the rest of the fence. The metal band was broken.

The ground shook and the strange carvings on the stone columns glowed and then went out. The demon and her children screamed, and then there was only silence. The demon children walked through the hole in the fence as she watched. Then they turned and watched as she slowly walked through the gap, and away from the prison that had held her for hundreds of years. She nodded her head to her children, signaling them to attack and kill the remaining men.

There was gunfire and screaming, and the remaining guards fought bravely, but in the end, it didn't take long before they all were dead.

She stood in front of the backhoe and Randall, "Get out."

"You promised not to hurt me or my men," he said.

"You humans trust too much, now get out."

He brought the arm of the backhoe down on her, in one last attempt to kill her. It was too little too late.

She picked herself off the ground and pointed to the cab where Randall was sitting. All the little creatures swarmed the cab, pulled open the door, and entered the cab. Randall was trapped. He tried reaching for his gun, but was too slow. The creatures attacked, and soon blood covered the inside of the windows and Randall stopped screaming.

She was free at last. Somehow even the air smelled better to her on the outside. The first order of things she had to do was to take care of some unfinished business. She looked at the fence from the outside, and she liked this view better. So many years wasted behind that fence, she thought to herself. The red mist flowed outside the fence line and covered all the dead bodies. When it receded back toward the temple, it took all the dead bodies with it, all but Randall's. There wasn't enough left of him to take back; only bits and pieces. It was like he was never there.

Lilith walked past the two tombstones. She remembered that day long ago and what had trapped her here; those two old men and the angel had tricked her, but she had made sure they all had paid the price for that. She should have killed all the people she found in the temple those years ago, if she had, she wouldn't have been trapped. It was a mistake she wouldn't repeat. They all must die this time.

That little extra time that Randall took in tearing down the fence was just enough time for Brett, Helen and Abraham to get away. Abraham remembered an old country church that was just a few miles from the old homestead, and hoped it was still there. He thought they would be safe there. He remembered something about holy land and that the demons didn't like it and couldn't pass through it. He didn't know how much time they had before the demon would find them. He knew better then to believe her when she said she would leave the area once she was free.

The church had been long since abandoned, and they had to break down the wooden door to get inside. Not much was left of the church now, just a few pews and a wooden altar.

Abraham remembered coming to this church as a young boy. It looked a lot different back then. It was one of the places that he always felt comfortable and safe in.

They brought their gear and supplies in and set up camp. There was no electricity, so they got the fireplace going for some heat and light, and set up a couple of lanterns that would come in handy. It would be getting dark soon.

They were at a loss for words. They figured the demon was loose by now, and they had no idea what to do next about it.

Helen decided she was going to send her crew back home in the morning, no use putting any more people in danger. She wanted them as far away from this place as possible. She still hoped they could find out what the markings on the stone columns meant. If they could find their meaning, she was sure it would help them put an end to this nightmare. There was just no more time to figure it out.

Abraham had retold the story of the day his father died and the last words the demon had told him; never trust a demon you fool, never trust a demon.

They heard the demon screaming Abraham's name. She stood outside the front door of the church.

That was when the lightning started. They could see her outline; her arms raised as the lightning flashed behind her. It was one hell of a scary sight.

She yelled, "We have unfinished business, Abraham. Give him to me, and I will let the rest be."

"We've heard that from you before," Brett said, "and we see how good your word is. We're going to stop you and send you back hell where you belong."

"What chance do you think you have against me? I will destroy all of you." She tried sending her children into the church, but they couldn't get through the door. Each time they tried, they were thrown backwards in a blinding white lite. It seemed that neither her, nor her children, could be on holy ground.

Abraham had everyone form a circle and hold hands. They prayed, over and over again, knowing she couldn't touch them while they were inside the church.

Lilith started to back away, "The hour grows late, you can't stay in there forever. I will return for you later." And then she was gone. She left her children there to guarding the group. They screamed and threw stones at the church all night, trying to get a reaction from the people who were trapped in the church.

Brett knew they would be safe if they all stayed inside and waited for the morning sun. "I'm not a big believer in religion, but I have to admit it felt good when we all held hands and prayed."

"I think we're safe now," said Abraham. "We need to hold out till daylight. If we can do that, we have a chance. The creatures will leave just before dawn."

"I'll take first watch," Brett said. "The rest of you try to get some sleep; it's going to be a long day tomorrow." He wasn't sure how much sleep the others would get, he knew he wouldn't be able to get any. He knew he would be heading back to the temple in the morning. He didn't know why, but he had a good feeling about what tomorrow would bring. Randall's words kept coming back to him. "What can you do that we haven't done," he had said. There had to be something we missed, Brett thought to himself. He just couldn't put his finger on it.

Lilith's children kept trying to get them to leave the old church, and just as Abraham had predicted, they left just before dawn.

They seemed to just vanish.

Abraham remembered what the angel had told him; that help would come when they needed it most. He wondered how much worse this could get before help arrived. He wondered what type of help they were going to get. He thought about telling the others about his dream, but decided against it. He had promised to keep it a secret, and Abraham was good at keeping secrets. He would be glad when this story came to an end and there would be no more secrets.

Back at the hospital, Cassie was having troubling thoughts; something wasn't right. The first thing she noticed was that the guards were still gone. They had left yesterday and hadn't returned. She figured that idiot government man had released the demon. She wondered if the demon had killed everyone left at the farm. She hoped that if she got free, she would leave the area, but she knew better than that.

She remembered reading in that old book about how the demon had first appeared on the farm over a hundred and fifty years ago. She knew that something was keeping the demon around; she just didn't know what that was. She wondered what had happened to her new friends Helen and Brett. She sure hoped they were OK. She had grown quite found of them and was worried about them. If what she read in that old book was true, they were going to have a tough go of it.

She got in her wheelchair and headed up to Fred's room. Fred was in a deep sleep. He was dreaming about his wife and son; they were all sitting on the porch swing drinking lemonade and watching the sun go down. He missed them so much.

Cassie looked at Fred lying helpless and hurt, she thought to herself, "Fred is such a good man. I couldn't have picked a better son-in-law myself." She loved him like he was her own son.

Cassie couldn't shake that bad feeling, and decided to stay in Fred's room to watch over him till sunrise. She learned long ago to trust her feelings. She wasn't there long, when she noticed that the temperature was dropping in the room.

The demon appeared at the end of Fred's bed. This was the first time she had ever seen demon. Her essence filled the room. Cassie had never felt so much evil and hate before. She was determined that the demon would not hurt her son-in-law.

The demon floated around the room, staring at Fred. She thought to herself, "He looks different from when I took his arm. Has it really been sixty years?"

Then, a bright light surrounded Fred and pushed Lilith back away from the bed and against the wall.

Lilith's eyes got very big. "This can't be," she said.

Standing next to his bed were Sarah and Jacob. "You can't take him," Sarah said, "we won't let you. Your time is almost over here. You should go and make the most best of it."

"What do you mean, my time is almost over? You can't stop me," the demon said. "I'm here to finish some old business. I took his arm the first time we met, and now I'm going to take his life. You're not strong enough to stop me. I will send him to a place that neither of you can get to. He will spend eternity feeling nothing but pain and sorrow."

Sarah looked into her eyes and said, "That's not going to happen."

"They can't stop you, but I can," said Cassie.

Lilith was surprised to hear Cassie speak. The crazy old women had been sitting in her wheelchair so silently.

The smile disappeared from Lilith's face, as Cassie came out of her chair running and screaming toward Lilith. Lilith had no time to react as Cassie wrapped her arms around Lilith and drove her through the third floor window. Cassie held her arms around Lilith and screamed at her while falling down all three floors; only stopping when they hit the ground.

"Foolish old woman," said Lilith looking down at Cassie's body, "you can't hurt me. You died for nothing." Lilith looked up toward the window and saw Sarah and Jacob there with a bright light behind them. Soon, a younger looking Cassie joined them.

Lilith watched in horror as the bright light spread to the rest of the hospital. Soon the whole place was bathed in light. She remembered seeing that light many years ago; the day she was trapped. The angel had helped them. She knew she couldn't get past the light to finish Fred. He would have to wait for another day.

Things weren't working out for her. First, she couldn't get Abraham out of the church, and now this. All at once, there was an uncontrollable urge pulling her back to the temple. She couldn't fight it. This was confusing to her. She didn't understand what was going on. She thought it had to be that damn curse the old witch put on her. "Tomorrow I will bring back that old witch and have her remove it. Then I will take care of these trouble makers and be free again."

It would be dawn soon, and she needed to rest. She slowly drifted back to the Smith farm.

Back at the old church, the demon's children had roamed around outside all night. We really couldn't understand what they were saying; it was just a bunch of mumbling and screaming. I don't know if they were trying to get at us or just trying to keep us from leaving. The last of them left just before dawn.

I let the others sleep, and had kept watch all night. I was hoping that the fence could be repaired and we could get the demon back inside somehow. If we couldn't figure out a way, they would all probably be killed. There just had to be a way to stop her.

The demon made it back to the temple. She was troubled by the events of the last twenty four hours. She knew the presence she had felt earlier was the angels. She was sure they would try to stop her. "Let them try," she thought to herself. "I destroyed one before, and I can do it again. And I have my children to help me this time. Let them come. I will be ready this time." She knew she would have to bring Gabriele back to lift the curse. She thought she would save her for last; the old witch had been more trouble then she'd been worth, and after tomorrow, she wouldn't matter anymore.

Abraham thought to himself, "So, it all came down to this-- one last stand." During the long dark night, Abraham had started to question his belief in his own religion. How could God let these demons wander the earth and cause so much pain and sorrow? Maybe this was God's way of testing us. No, he didn't believe much of that *testing us* theory that he was taught. And then it came to him—how could they believe in one and not the other? God, the devil and humans were all tied together in some way. They had been since man first set foot on earth. Maybe the three need each other in order balance things out. Who knew? The one thing he did know was his belief in God.

Abraham was thinking about his father and how much he loved and respected him. He knew none of the people here right now had brought this evil to this place, but it was going to be up to them to put a stop to it. He thought it had been strange, those sixty years ago, that his father walked through the gate to face the demon. He understood now.

Brett was a realist. He knew they had no chance in stopping the demon tomorrow, but he was willing to try, and if he had to, he would die for the cause.

Helen had her eyes shut, but couldn't sleep. All the things she had gone through her whole life had led up to this, and she was scared and excited at the same time. This was way beyond the ghost studies she had done. She wondered why when she was young and could see and talk to ghosts that the subject of demons never came up. She realized the demon was right, that she didn't know all that much about the demon's world and how it was connected to the human world. If she lived through this, she was going to make sure she corrected that.

Day Six

During the night the hospital staff had moved Fred to another room while they fixed the window. They had a hard time understanding how or why a crippled old woman had thrown herself out the window and killed herself. Many people at the hospital thought she was worried that Fred would die and that she would be left alone or end up in an old people's home. Others thought that she just couldn't stand all the grief she had faced in her lifetime, and that what was happening to Fred pushed her over the edge.

It was too bad they would never know how much she loved her son-in-law and how she gave her life to protect him.

When they were cleaning her room, they found the letter she had written to Fred before she died. The nurses all gathered around as one of them read the letter out load, there wasn't a dry eye among them. When she finished reading it, and they all understood the love between the members of the Smith family, they decided she wasn't just a scary old lady after all.

Fred's vitals were all over the place since they moved him to the new room. The doctors believed that to be a sign that he would soon come out of his coma.

Something was tugging on Fred's arm as he woke to a voice that he hadn't heard for a long time, "Wake up, Sleepy Head," and "Come on, Dad, you have to get up." There next to his bed were Sarah and Jacob. Standing behind them was Cassie; looking like she did when she was much younger. "Is this a dream or am I dead," Fred asked Sarah.

"Heavens no," she said. "It's not your time. There's work you need to finish at the farm. You need to help your friends put an end to this nightmare."

"Friends? What friends? I don't have any."

"Stop talking like that, Fred," Sarah said, "and you have more friends than you know. They have been, and will always be, there for you when you need them. But, I have some bad news, Fred. The demon escaped from the farm and came here looking for you last night. The three of us drove her away. Cassie gave her life last night protecting you. That's why she's here with us now. The demon will come after you again, if you don't stop her. Fred, she has to be stopped. It's the only way to save yourself and the town, and end the curse."

"I don't want to go back to the farm. I want to stay here with you. I've given my life protecting the secret and that dammed temple, and I'm tired."

Sarah smiled at Fred. "All I want is for this to be over so we can be together again, but you have to go back, Fred. It has to be finished. We will all be together again, but it won't be any time soon. We are always in your heart and you will always be in ours. Your friends will be meeting you at the farm. You have to hurry."

Fred found his clothes and quickly dressed. "I miss you so much."

"I know," she said, "just remember...we will always be with you, and we will all be a family again someday."

He turned toward his smiling family and they faded away.

For the first time in years, the darkness in his soul was gone. It was like a weight had been lifted from his shoulders. He was sad about Cassie's passing. She had been like a mother to him. He knew she was in a better place, with people who loved her. She had struggled and suffered for many years after her stroke.

A new determination took over; someone was going to pay for her death, and he walked out of the hospital.

The hospital staff had tried unsuccessfully to stop him. He was a tough old man.

There's something special about watching the sun come up in the country; the way the sun hits the fields, the way the birds start flying around, and the dew lays on the grass. I felt a little strange as we gathered for another set of prayers. I have never been much of a religious man, but it seemed the right thing to do this morning. The sun was shining through what was left of the stained glass windows of the old church. It was almost as if God was there with us, joining us in the prayers that made a believer out of me.

We said a tearful goodbye to Helen's crew and watched as they drove away. They didn't want to leave, but knew there was nothing they could do here anymore. They would head back to the university and wait to hear from us.

"One last thing before we go, Abraham said. He took out a small vial of holy water and made the sign of the cross on each of our foreheads.

"Do you think that will help us?" I asked.

"Don't know," said Abraham, "but it sure can't hurt. Besides, I always wanted to do that."

We got into my cruiser then, and started back toward the farm. We took one last look at the old church, and for the first time, noticed the name of the church, Sunrise Country Church. It was the church that Samuel built a hundred and fifty years ago.

"Just think about that, the man who had helped trap the demon all those years ago, had built a church that had saved our lives last night--over a hundred years after he had died." That fact alone made Brett start thinking that there might be something to this religious thing, and that they might have a chance after all.

Fred was the first to arrive at his farm. He was surprised, and mad, at what he saw when he drove up. There were several cars and lots of equipment scattered around the farm. He thought it was strange that there weren't any people there. He wondered if that damn demon was still around. He didn't know what to think about the three helicopters sitting in his corn field. He just shook his head. He didn't know what had been happening here, and was sure it wasn't good.

He went into the house and retrieved his shotgun. He took one last look around the house. He had spent his whole life here. He was born here, was raised here, and the way it was going, he would probably die here. He looked at the pictures of his wife and son. He kissed his fingers and touched their faces. God, he missed them.

One way or another, he knew this would end today, and for that he was thankful. He was walking out the front door when Brett's car pulled into the driveway and up to the house.

Fred smiled as he saw his old friends, Abraham and Brett. It had been sixty years since he had seen Abraham, but he recognized him immediately. Everything came flooding back to him about the day Sam climbed over that woodpile.

He remembered Sam climbing over the fence. He was always a better climber. He remembered it like it was yesterday, as Sam fell off the top of the fence and landed on the inside. Sam had been laughing as he got to his feet and dusted himself off.

Then that strange woman appeared behind him and grabbed him by the shirt collar. Fred reached through the fence with his right arm, trying to help his friend, and then he remembered the terrible pain as he felt his arm being torn off.

The next thing he remembered was Abraham putting something around his arm and telling him to lie still. He remembered Abraham's father opening the gate and going inside to help Sam, and then watching as she killed the two of them. The next thing he remembered was waking up in the hospital with his dad by his side. Sometimes, memories can be a painful thing. It was time to let it all go now.

No words were spoken they all just headed down that dirt road to the temple. They were shocked at what they found there. The backhoe was close to the broken down fence with what was left of Randall's body still inside. The ghost hunters' van was still parked by the edge of the fence. Hard to believe this all happened because one man refused to take the advice of the sheriff. The only thing missing were the bodies, and they were all gone.

They remembered the old story about the mist taking the bodies when it retreated back into the ground and wondered if that was what happened to them. The smell was worse today, and it seemed to be getting stronger as they approached the temple.

The area around the temple looked different today. It appeared as though several trees outside the fence line had died overnight. Whatever was inside the fence was now spreading out and taking over the whole area.

After looking at the damage Randall had done, they knew they couldn't repair the fence. They had neither the time nor tools to get it done, and even if they could have, they had no way of getting the demon back inside.

Fred looked at the others and asked Helen about the stone columns with the marking on them. She said they knew who had made them, but didn't know what the symbols meant. All she knew was that it trapped the demon inside the fence for hundreds of years.

He wondered if he broke one into several small pieces, and loaded them into his shotgun, if they would have any effect on her.

Helen didn't know. But thought it was worth a try. They also took several pieces of the metal fence and made spears out of them. It was the first positive thing they had thought of for stopping the demon since this all started. It was almost funny that something so simple might help them destroy the demon. Could this be the missing piece that they had been looking for?

There was one stone that was larger than the rest. Instead of lettering on it, there was a cross symbol. They looked at all the other columns and found that it was the only one with that symbol, which had to mean something.

Brett was helping Fred break up some of the smaller stone columns into pieces and packing them into the shotgun shells. Every time the hammer hit the stones, the letters glowed. Hopefully, that was a good sign.

Helen and Abraham looked for more clues; anything at all that would help them. That's when she noticed the shape of the fence line. No one had noticed it before, but it was shaped like a cross with the temple right at the center of it. It made sense to her that the angel would trap the demon inside the cross.

Time went by slowly that morning. They could almost hear each tick of the clock.

Fred said he had been worried about who would watch over the temple once he was gone, so maybe it was the right time for this to happen.

Around one o'clock, the wind picked up and the clouds move in. So much for a nice, sunny day, Brett thought.

Around three, the group noticed movement inside the fenced area, and the red mist started seeping from the ground.

The first to appear were the little creatures. There were perhaps ten of them. They stood by the torn down gate.

Before they made their move, Fred shot at them. It seemed the stones worked better than any of the bullets that were fired at them. The first shot took two out. They screamed and seemed to turn to dust. They made one more charge, but quickly backed away when Fred took out three more. They retreated back inside the temple.

"What have you done to my children? You know that won't work on me," the demon said. She had appeared directly in front of them. "Fred and Abraham, I'm glad you're both here. I was going to hunt you both down and kill you today. You saved me the trouble of finding you. And Fred, you are going to pay for hurting my children." She screamed and made her way toward them.

Fred fired at her, and she didn't even slow down.

Brett and Helen threw the makeshift spears at her. One of them hit her arm, and they could tell that Lilith was in pain as she backed away. All of a sudden, there were several lighting strikes and thunder rumbled over the old stone temple, the force of which knocked them all down. An old woman walked out of the temple.

Lilith turned and looked at her and said, "You're not supposed to be here. I haven't called for you. How did you come back?"

The old woman stood face to face with the demon and said, "You're not the only one that has power. You seem to have forgotten that I'm a witch. This isn't why I summoned you all those years ago. I wanted you to help my people, and to take revenge for their deaths. All these people have had nothing to do with that. All they are doing is protecting their own; the same as I was all those years ago. You have gone too far this time."

"So this is how you repay me for killing your enemy's, by turning against me?"

Gabriele said, "I should have stopped you when you killed those people that trapped you here."

Lilith laughed and said, "What makes you think you could have stopped me, you silly old witch?"

Gabriele walked over to the old tombstones, looked at Brett, and said, "I'm sorry for all the pain I have caused. It wasn't supposed to be this way. I only wanted revenge on the soldiers who murdered my people." She dropped to her knees and started chanting in a language that none of them had heard before.

Lilith walked up behind her. "They deserved everything that happened to them for tricking and trapping me here," she said to Gabriele.

"No, they didn't," was the old witches reply. "I knew I couldn't trust you, that's why I put a spell on you and this place. The spell only took effect if you came back here. You just couldn't help yourself, could you? When you saw the Smiths move onto the land, you had to show up, didn't you? That's when the curse started; when you came back and killed the elder Smith man. Why didn't you stay away from this place after you killed the soldiers? None of this would have happened, if you had just stayed away."

"You stupid witch. No one tells me where I can go and what I can do. They had no right to build that temple on land that you yourself cursed. My only mistake that day was letting any of them live. I should have killed them all."

"When you killed the angel, you angered the sprits that live here. They will never let you go. You may be free of the cage, but you never will be free of this place. You will always have to return here by dawn each day. The sprits are more powerful than you. You have no choice in the matter."

"Do you know how far I can go in a day, Witch? And how many people I can kill before I have to return here? If I'm trapped here, I will take my wrath out on every living thing I can. I shall have my freedom, and my revenge. My master will never let you keep me here. Talk to the sprits Gabriele, make them understand. Convince them to release me, and I will go far away and never return."

"That will never happen, Demon. You have no place in the world anymore. It's already underway. If you thought the cage was bad, wait till you see what they have in in store for you."

"No," screamed the demon, "once I kill all of you, I will be free of this place. My master will see to it that I'm free."

"Your master isn't the most powerful being in the universe, even you know that. After today, you will never be free of this place," said Gabriele, and she started chanting.

"We shall see," and with that, Lilith laid her hands on Gabriele's shoulder.

Gabriele stopped chanting and looked toward Brett. "Be brave. It will soon be over." She slowly turned to dust.

Brett's group watched as Gabriele's body broke apart and fell to the ground. The wind picked up and blew the dust that had once been Gabriele into the swamp.

"So much for her," Lilith said and turned her attention to the remaining people.

All at once the ground shook, and the bodies of old preacher and the medicine man rose up through the ground and appeared behind their tombstones.

"Why are you here? Did that old witch summon you? It won't matter. I killed you centuries ago, and I will kill you again."

"You no longer have any power over us, Demon," the medicine man said, "and yes, the old witch did summon us. We're back to finish the job we started long ago.

She tried to grab them, but her hands went right threw them. Each time she tried to touch them, her arms started bleeding. This was new for her. She never before felt this kind of pain. After several attempts to kill the two religious men, she ran screaming into the temple to get away from them.

"We have to hurry," the old preacher said. "We don't have much time." He asked Fred to dig a hole in the earth, and to fill it again, when he was told.

"I can do that." Fred got in the backhoe, pulled what was left of Randall's body out, and started digging a hole just outside of where the old fence gate used to be.

"The rest of you form a circle and join in prayer with us. Don't let go, no matter what happens. Keep praying and don't break the circle." The two sprits joined hands with Abraham, Helen and Brett, and started praying out loud.

Fred had the hole dug to about ten feet deep when the screaming started again.

Lilith floated out the door and toward the group. "I may not be able to touch you two, but I can still kill them."

Fred jumped out of the backhoe with his shotgun and shot the remaining demon's children.

The demon stopped for a moment, and looked at him. "I will save you for last. You will have a terrible death for what you did to my children." She turned toward the group. "I will never let you keep me here. I will destroy all of you." She was floating a couple of feet off the ground. "I will start with you, Ghost Hunter. You're going to see firsthand what being a ghost is really like," and then she headed straight for Helen.

Brett pushed Helen out of the way. As Lilith reached the circle of people, he pulled out his gun and emptied the clip into her.

"Haven't you learned by now that your bullets can't hurt me?"

Brett threw his gun at her and then charged her; driving her away from the group of praying people. He tried a couple of moves that he had learned in the army.

She quickly overpowered him, wrapping her arms around him. Brett was trapped. In one last attempt to free himself, he head butted the demon. All that did was piss her off. She looked into his eyes and said, "So you want to be the first to die? So be it. The others will soon follow." She had him in a bear hug and slowly squeezed the life out of him. She opened her arms, and Brett's body fell to the ground dead.

Laughing, she said, "Who's next? I think I will start with you, Abraham. I want you to feel the same pain as your father did before he died.

"That's not going to happen," said Abraham as the remaining people reformed the circle and began praying again. The stone columns stared glowing and bright lights came out of the sky. Helen, Fred and Abraham were blinded for a second, and when they opened their eyes, there were three angels standing between them and Lilith. It was then that Abraham understood the meaning of his dream. The angel's wings spread wide, and their swords were draw. "Keep praying," one of them said to circle of friends. "We need to put an end to this."

Although she had killed one angel, she knew she had no chance against three. They encircled her, and slowly pushed her back toward the hole Fred had dug.

They stopped when she was next to the stone with the strange symbol on it. They joined hands and spoke in a strange language and the symbol started glowing. Lilith was slowly sucked into the stone. She screamed, "You can't do this to me," till the last of her disappeared into the stone.

"Maybe we can't kill you, but we can trap you in this cross shaped stone." The angels then turned toward the group, "No human can ever touch this stone," one of the angels said, and Fred used the backhoe to push it into the hole and cover it with dirt.

Helen broke the circle and ran toward Brett's body. She lifted his head onto her lap and slowly brushed his hair.

The angels told Abraham that he had kept his faith, and that no one must ever learn of the location of the stone. They turned toward Fred and said that his duty was done now, and that he could leave this place. Without saying another word, the angels vanished. The sun broke through the clouds and the whole temple site was bathed in sunlight; and just like that, it felt like all the evil left the place.

A little boy with a strange white glow around him walked out of the temple toward Helen and kneeled next to Brett's body. He laid both of his hands on his chest.

Brett started gasping for breath, and then his eyes opened. "We're not ready for you yet," said little boy, "there is much work to be done."

"Are you God?" asked Brett. The boy smiled and said, "No. I'm your uncle, Sam."

"What am I supposed to do now?" he asked.

"Whatever's in your heart," said Sam. The little boy looked at Fred and said, "I have missed you, my old friend."

"I'm sorry that I didn't help you all those years ago," Fred said.

"There was nothing you could have done. Abraham, your father wanted me to tell you he loves you very much, and he's very proud of the man you have become. You have paid a heavy price for guarding the secret temple for all these years, you are all free now. Live your lives to the fullest till we meet again. All of you have done well today. It's time for me go now. Take heart on what you have accomplished today." He walked back into the temple and was never seen again.

Helen helped Brett to his feet. Confused, Brett asked what had happened.

"The sprits have favored you," the old medicine replied, "they must have a plan for you. No one should ever learn what's buried here. The temple and the fence should be torn down and buried so no one will ever know it existed. The road should be blocked off so that nature can reclaim this place. The land will heal itself. In a few years, no one will ever recognize this place. The death stone well remain buried deep in the middle of the swamp for all time. There will be many people coming here soon, and you can never tell anyone about the buried stone or what's inside it. The rest is up to you what you tell the others. No one will believe you, but you can try. It's time for us to go now and rejoin our families." The two old friends walked down the dirt path, away from the temple, and by the time they had reached the end of the clearing, they were gone.

The four friends sat together on one of the stone columns.

Fred looked at Abraham and said, "So it's finally over and the demon can never cause any harm again. It's been a long time coming."

The group looked around their surroundings and noticed that everything had changed. The trees around the swamp looked like they had come back to life, and there were even birds in the trees.

"What do we do now?" Brett asked.

"Well, I could use a cold beer," said Abraham.

They all laughed and started walking back toward the Smith farmhouse.

The ghosts were right. Several government men showed up later that day and took us all into what they called *protective custody*. Poor Abraham didn't get his cold beer. At least not that day.

They separated us and asked a lot of dumb questions for about two weeks. They didn't believe anything we told them.

At first, they accused us of being terrorists and told us we were going to be sent to foreign prisons and held forever. They were trying to scare us into a confession. It didn't work.

After going through what we did this last week, it would have taken more than that to scare us. After about two weeks, they started to change their tone. They tried to convince us that we all were drugged and brainwashed. That didn't work either, and in the end, we were all brought into a large room and told that a group of terrorists were responsible for all of this, and that the reality show group had stumbled on them by accident and were killed. They went on to explain that Charlie and his deputies, and the highway patrol men were also killed by them when they went to investigate. We were told that they had some chemical weapons and that some of them had leaked and had contaminated the bodies, and because of that, all the bodies had to be destroyed for safety's sake. There was no mention of Randall, or how his men had been killed.

They finally released us, and the government gave Helen a large grant to further her studies in the supernatural. They wanted her to work for them as a consultant from time to time; they had closed down the office of paranormal research that Randall had worked in.

When they took their equipment off Fred's farm, they forgot the backhoe and bulldozer. They had it all cleaned up and repainted before they left, and they also left a check for two-hundred and fifty thousand dollars for damage they had done to his farm.

Abraham got a new roof and windows for his church, due to an unknown donation of one-hundred thousand dollars to the church.

The Church Point sheriff's department was given five brand new patrol cars, along with the latest new weapons and equipment.

About a month after the incident, a group from the television station showed up looking for their van and equipment. They were all screaming about freedom of the press and how they were going to sue everybody, and that they thought it was strange that nobody could find the van. The next time I saw Fred, he told me he'd buried it someplace on his land. He'd made good use out of the backhoe and bulldozer.

Before the TV crew left town, they checked in on Kathy at the hospital; turns out she had a complete breakdown and had been sent to the asylum. They didn't know if she would ever get out.

We told our story to the people who would listen. Not many believed us. They believed we had been drugged; most of them thought it was a bad LSD experience.

A bond had formed between those of us who survived that week together; one that would remain for the rest of our lives. Abraham flew back home to his church, but promised he would return the following spring. Helen drove back to her university in Baton Rouge with the same promise. Before she left, she whispered in my ear that she still had a copy of the video that was taken that first day, and that she was saving it for a rainy day. She kissed me on the cheek and walked out of my life. Fred used the backhoe and tore down what was left of the fence and temple. What he couldn't bury, he pushed into the swamp. He smiled as he did it. He knew the EPA and the watershed district and about ten other government agencies would be pissed about that part, and that made him happy. The last thing he did was take out the road leading to the old temple site so no-one could ever get back there again. He used the money the government had given him to fix up the old homestead. It now looked like it did thirty years ago, before Sarah and Jacob died. Last I talked to him, he was thinking about selling his farm and heading up to Canada to visit his long lost relatives.

People started to believe the story the government had passed around, about it being a group of terrorists that had caused all the problems. I think most people around here knew there was more to the story than that, but had decided to let sleeping dogs sleep. I still get asked about it from time to time, and I tell most of them I just can't remember much about it. Truth be told, most people don't want to talk about demons, so I just stopped telling them about it.

Every week millions of people pray to gods they have never seen. I guess I'm a believer now, and yes, I sleep with the lights on and a gun under my pillow.

Did I mention that Fred and I kept a couple of the stone columns from the fence? We broke them into little pieces and loaded them into our gun shells. You can never be too careful.

About the Author

As a boy I spent a lot of time at the movies, back then they had a Saturday afternoon double feature horror and monster movies. I remember that I was given a fifty cent allowance for the week and with that I could get into the movies, buy a pop and a candy bar. Some things have changed since then but I still love going to the movies and you guessed it horror movies are my favorite. I worked in construction for most of my life and when I turned sixty I had a stroke, part of my therapy was to write, I had always wanted to write but never took the time. I had some story ideas that I thought were pretty good so I started writing; turns out I love to write. I have a new found respect for writers it might be the hardest thing I have ever done. Time will tell if other people like my stories. For now, I'm a Sixty-two year old, soon to be retired construction worker, that loves to write horror stories and it doesn't bother me one bit that I don't have to go outside in the cold Minnesota winter.

CPSIA information can be obtained
at www.ICGtesting.com
Printed in the USA
LVOW01*2305121115

462029LV00006B/21/P